ISLE OF LIES AND LEGENDS

THE FORGOTTEN ISLE SAGA
BOOK 0.5

MCCAYLEIGH DANIELS

First published in the United States in 2025

ISBN-13:
Paperback: 979-8-9915192-2-9
Hardcover: 979-8-9915192-3-6

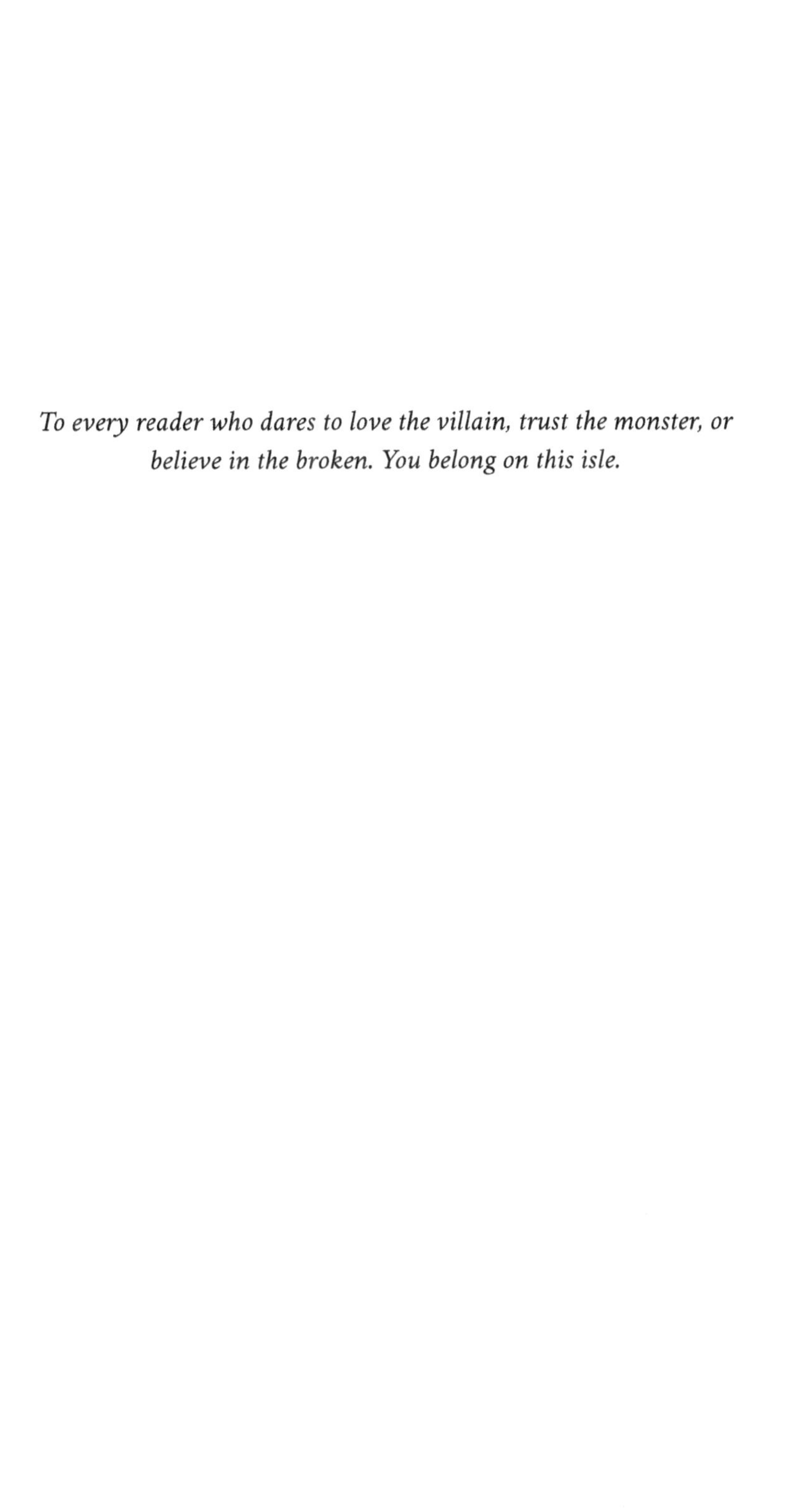

To every reader who dares to love the villain, trust the monster, or believe in the broken. You belong on this isle.

ABOUT THE BOOK

While this book is classified as Young Adult and contains no overly explicit scenes, there are still some topics that may be sensitive to certain readers. For your awareness, a full list of trigger warnings can be found at the back of the book.

Shadowspeak
Valoria
Kingdom of Aurian
Oxreach
Aramore
Alverstone
Kingdom of Eldaraya
Mount Vorel
N
W
E
S

Edros
The Isle

PART I

CONIVX

The sea was a monster with no mercy.

It roared and foamed, an endless maw of churning black water, swallowing everything in its path. The ship was gone—splintered, devoured. The wreckage bobbed like shattered bones upon the waves, the storm still raging overhead.

Conivx's fingers ached as she clung to a jagged piece of debris, her knuckles bloodless, her body screaming with exhaustion. The salt stung her raw skin, filled her nose, her mouth, as the ocean dragged her down, again and again, like a beast playing with its prey.

A strangled cry barely reached her ears over the howling winds.

"Vespera!"

She twisted, heart hammering. Through the slashing rain, her sister's form flickered in and out of sight, tossed like a broken doll amidst the waves. Her amber eyes, wide with terror, locked onto Conivx's.

"I can't—" Vespera gasped, her fingers clawing at the water, reaching.

Another wave rose like a towering wall, crashing between them, stealing her away.

No.

With a guttural scream, Conivx lunged forward, slicing through the freezing water, her muscles burning, lungs seizing. She kicked, pulled, fought. The sea was an unrelenting force, dragging her back, pressing against her like a living, vengeful thing.

But she wouldn't lose Vespera.

Her fingers brushed wet skin, then bone-thin wrists. She grabbed hold, her grip iron, just as the next wave crashed over them.

The world became a violent nothingness—foam and darkness, salt and pain.

Down. Down.

Pressure crushed her ribs. Her lungs screamed for air. Vespera's wrist began to slip.

Not this time.

With every ounce of strength she had left, Conivx kicked upward, dragging them both toward the faint, fractured light above. The ocean fought her, pulling them back, unwilling to give up its prey. But she was done losing.

Just when her vision blurred to black, the sea spat them out.

The impact was a shock—jagged rocks, wet sand, the raw burn of air in her lungs. Conivx barely registered the sting of scraping flesh before she collapsed onto her hands and knees, coughing up seawater, sucking in oxygen like it was the first breath she'd ever taken.

For a moment, there was only the ragged sound of her breathing, the distant roar of the tide.

Then she remembered.

"Vespera."

Her voice was hoarse, barely a whisper, but she forced herself to move, to crawl toward the unmoving form beside her.

Vespera lay sprawled on the wet shore, her golden-brown hair tangled with sand, her skin deathly pale.

No. No, no, no—

Conivx grabbed her by the shoulders, shaking her roughly. "Vespera!"

A heartbeat of silence. Then—a violent cough, a sharp gasp.

Vespera turned onto her side, hacking up seawater, her body shuddering. Conivx slumped back, breath hitching between exhaustion and relief.

"Conivx?" Vespera rasped, blinking up at her.

A lump formed in Conivx's throat, but she swallowed it down. "Who else would I be?"

Vespera attempted a weak smile, though it faltered as she took in their surroundings. "Where... where are we?"

Conivx followed her gaze, unease curling like a snake in her stomach.

The coastline stretched in either direction, jagged and uninviting. The sand was dark, almost gray, littered with driftwood and broken shells. Beyond the beach, the land rose sharply into cliffs, shrouded in thick, rolling mist. The air carried a biting chill, though the season should have been warm.

Something about this place felt... wrong.

Not just unfamiliar. Not just dangerous.

Wrong.

Conivx pushed herself up, muscles trembling from exhaustion. "I don't know," she admitted.

Vespera, still weak, reached for her hand, seeking reassurance. "At least we're alive," she murmured. "We'll figure this out together, won't we?"

Conivx nodded, but a hollow feeling gnawed at her.

Together.

Vespera had always been the beloved one. The one people trusted, admired. Even now, half-drowned and trembling, she looked untouchable—like something out of a legend, a tragic heroine who would emerge from this stronger than before.

And Conivx?

Conivx was the reason they had been exiled from their kingdom.

Her magic. Her ambition.

But there was power here. She could feel it, pulsing beneath her feet, coiling in the mist like a living thing.

A rustling in the undergrowth made Conivx stiffen. Her pulse quickened as shadowy figures emerged from the mist, their weathered faces flickering between caution and curiosity.

"By the gods," a gruff voice murmured. "Survivors."

The word felt like an accusation rather than relief. Conivx's dull eyes narrowed, assessing the newcomers with quiet suspicion. Beside her, Vespera, ever the peacemaker, offered a trembling smile, her damp curls clinging to her face.

"Please," Vespera said, her voice hoarse from salt and exhaustion. "We've been shipwrecked. Can you help us?"

An older woman stepped forward, her silver-streaked hair wild from the wind, her gnarled hands outstretched in an almost maternal gesture. "Of course, dears. You poor things look half-drowned. Come, let's get you to the village."

Conivx fought the instinct to recoil as rough hands reached to steady her. There was something wrong here—something in the very air, a quiet hum beneath her feet, a presence thick as the mist curling between the trees. A weight pressed down on her chest, not unlike the moment before a storm broke.

"Where are we?" she asked, her voice measured.

The villagers exchanged uneasy glances. Finally, the old woman answered, her voice thick with something unspoken. "This is the isle."

Conivx arched a brow. "The isle?"

"That's all it's ever been called," a younger man added, his hollow eyes unreadable. "It doesn't need another name. Few who come here ever leave."

Vespera hesitated, glancing at Conivx. They had no choice but to follow.

The path twisted through an ancient forest, the riot of the shore giving way to an unnatural silence. Conivx exhaled slowly, steadying herself. She had lost everything—her home, her status, her place in Aurian. But maybe, just maybe, she could rebuild something here.

Ahead, nestled in the valley, the village emerged from the gloom. Ramshackle cottages leaned against one another, their thatched roofs sagging under years of disrepair. Dim lanterns cast long, twitching shadows across the cobbled paths.

The old woman turned back to them, a tight smile stretching her lined face. "Welcome to your new home."

Home. The word rang hollow in Conivx's mind.

But this place was something else entirely. Something waiting.

Power lurked beneath the surface of this land.

And this time, no one—not Vespera, not the gods, not fate itself—would stand in her way.

As they stepped into the village center, the mist curled around their ankles, damp and clinging. The air felt heavy, thick with something unspoken. The villagers stood in wary clusters, their faces shadowed by flickering lanterns, their gazes a mixture of curiosity and unease.

Vespera, ever radiant despite their ordeal, stepped forward with a warm smile. Even with her damp curls clinging to her face, she looked composed, grateful.

"Thank you all for your kindness," she said, her voice smooth and soothing. "We're so grateful for your help."

The villagers' rigid stances eased. A weathered fisherman, his face lined with years of hardship, stepped forward hesitantly.

"Aye, lass. It's not often we see new faces 'round here," he said, though his gaze flickered past her to Conivx—cautious, uncertain. "Especially ones that survive the journey."

Conivx said nothing, her dark eyes scanning the crowd, noting every whisper and hesitant glance. She stood apart, her pale skin ghostly in the dim lantern glow.

"Tell me," she finally spoke, her voice measured, almost too calm. "What exactly lurks beyond your village borders?"

A heavy silence fell over them. The villagers exchanged uneasy looks, but before anyone could answer, Vespera laughed lightly, diffusing the tension with practiced ease.

"My sister, always the curious one," she said, gently touching Conivx's arm as if to pull her back from the edge. "Perhaps those tales are best saved for when we're rested, hmm?"

Conivx stiffened at the touch. Always the peacemaker. Always stealing the moment. Even here, even now, she was the one they trusted.

As Vespera continued talking, drawing them in as she always did, Conivx remained silent, watching. The air here was thick with something old, something powerful. She could feel it humming beneath her feet, coiling in the mist.

Power.

She would find it.

A hunched old woman stepped forward, her clouded eyes unreadable. "We've a small cottage on the outskirts," she rasped, pointing toward a narrow, winding path that disappeared into the mist. "It's not much, but it'll keep you dry."

Vespera's face brightened. "Oh, that's so kind of you! We couldn't possibly—"

"We accept," Conivx cut in sharply, her gaze locking onto the elder's. A slow, knowing smile played at her lips. "Your generosity won't be forgotten."

The old woman gave a slow nod.

As they walked the misty path, the village faded behind them, swallowed by the thick fog. The silence between them stretched.

Vespera's easy acceptance of charity grated on Conivx. She acted as if kindness alone could mend their broken fate, as if they hadn't lost everything.

The cottage loomed ahead—a squat, weathered structure of stone and thatch. Inside, it was sparse but dry. A small hearth, a rough-hewn bench, and a single bed.

Vespera let out a soft sigh of relief, brushing damp strands from her face. "It's not so bad, is it? We can make this work."

Conivx prowled the room, running her fingers along the uneven walls. "Make what work?" she asked, her voice edged with bitterness. "Our exile? Our fall from grace?"

Vespera flinched but didn't back down. "Con, please," she said. "We're alive. We're together. That's what matters."

Conivx gave a cold, humorless laugh. "Is it?" She turned, meeting her sister's eyes. "And how long before your new adoring public comes knocking, desperate for more of your boundless optimism?"

Vespera's face fell, hurt flashing in her amber eyes. "Why do you always do this?" Her voice wavered. "Why can't you just—"

"Just what?" Conivx snapped, stepping closer. "Pretend this is some grand adventure? That we haven't lost everything? That I didn't ruin us?"

Silence.

Vespera swallowed, her throat bobbing. "We haven't lost each other," she whispered.

For a moment, Conivx felt something stir—a flicker of

something raw. Regret, maybe. A memory of what they had once been.

But she crushed it.

Ambition rose like a tide, drowning everything else.

She turned away, her voice barely more than a whisper.

"No," she said. "I suppose we haven't. Yet."

2

The flickering candle cast grotesque shadows across the cottage walls as night descended upon the isle. The air inside was thick, heavy with the scent of damp wood and salt. Conivx lay awake, staring at the wavering flame, its glow catching in her dark eyes. Her raven hair spilled across the pillow like ink, a stark contrast to her pale skin.

Beside her, Vespera slumbered peacefully, her golden-brown tresses fanned out across the pillow, her features soft and serene. Even after everything—the wreck, the storm, their exile—Vespera looked untouched by misfortune, as if even fate itself hesitated to tarnish her.

Conivx's lips curled into a bitter smile.

"Even in sleep, you outshine me, dear sister," she whispered, her voice barely audible over the crackling wick.

The events of the day replayed in her mind, each moment sharpening the resentment that had long festered beneath her skin. The way the villagers had softened in Vespera's presence, how their wary glances had lingered on Conivx with suspicion.

Even here, in this forgotten place, Vespera had them under her spell.

Conivx clenched her fists beneath the threadbare blanket.

"Why?" she hissed, her whisper swallowed by the night. "Why is it always you?"

A shift in the bed. A breath, a sigh. Conivx froze, holding still as Vespera stirred before settling once more.

The silence stretched, thick and suffocating. And then, unbidden, a memory surfaced.

She saw herself in their family's grand hall, younger and full of quiet longing. Vespera, radiant as always, stood at the center of a circle of courtiers, their laughter ringing through the air.

"Vespera, you're simply marvelous!" one of them exclaimed. "How do you do it?"

Vespera's laughter was bright, effortless. "Oh, it's nothing, really. I just try to see the best in everyone."

Conivx lurked in the shadows, as she always had, watching.

"And what of your sister?" another voice asked. "Conivx, isn't it? She's so... different from you."

Vespera's expression softened. "Con is brilliant, truly," she said, as if speaking of some distant cousin rather than the sister who had always been at her side. "She just needs time to come out of her shell."

Time.

As if time could ever bridge the chasm between them.

The memory faded, leaving only the sting of it behind. Conivx exhaled slowly, her fingers uncurling.

She turned her gaze to Vespera's sleeping form, and in that moment, a decision crystallized within her. No longer would she stand in her sister's shadow. No longer would she be an afterthought.

"I will forge my own path," she vowed in silence. "And when

I am done, they will speak of Vespera as nothing more than Conivx's sister."

She rose from the bed, moving as fluid as a wraith. The floorboards didn't dare creak beneath her weight as she glided toward the door. Pausing at the threshold, she cast one last glance at Vespera's peaceful form.

Then she slipped out into the night.

The village lay shrouded in mist, a spectral landscape of shifting shadows and muffled sounds. The air carried the briny tang of the sea, mixing with the distant scent of damp earth. Conivx's steps were silent as she walked, her fingers trailing along the rough-hewn fences, feeling the uneven grain of the wood beneath her fingertips.

Something sparked within her at the sensation. A whisper of possibility.

"Power," she murmured, the word lingering on her tongue like a promise. "It's here, waiting to be claimed."

A stray cat slunk from an alley, its lean form cutting through the fog. It paused, watching her with wary, golden eyes, its back arched slightly in suspicion.

Conivx met its gaze, unblinking. In that moment, she understood it—the wariness, the hunger.

"You and I," she whispered, kneeling slowly, "we know what it's like to be unwanted."

The cat hissed, retreating into the darkness. Conivx smirked, a cold satisfaction curling in her chest.

As she reached the village's edge, the mist parted, revealing the land beyond. Twisted trees stood gnarled and ancient, their skeletal branches reaching skyward. Jagged rocks jutted from the earth, their surfaces slick with moisture. The air itself felt different here, charged with something old, something waiting.

Conivx's heart pounded—not with fear, but with something sharper.

Anticipation.

"This place," she thought, breath shallow, "it's not like home. Here, the old rules don't apply."

She closed her eyes, inhaling deeply, feeling the pulse of something ancient beneath her feet. It hummed in the earth, in the air, in the silence.

When she opened her eyes again, her expression was no longer hesitant. It was resolute.

"I will bend this island to my will," she whispered, her words lost to the wind.

A sudden gust swept through the clearing, cold and sharp, sending a shiver down her spine. It carried with it the scent of rain, of damp stone, of something deeper, more secret. The mist shifted, curling around her ankles, as if drawn to her presence.

As if it, too, was waiting.

Conivx turned her gaze toward the darkness beyond the village, her pulse thrumming in her ears.

She had been cast aside before. She had been overlooked, underestimated.

But here, on this forsaken isle, she would rise.

And for the first time in her life, Vespera's light would not be the one that shone the brightest.

Tendrils of mist coiled around Conivx's ankles as she wandered through the sleeping village, her footsteps muffled by the dense fog. She hadn't meant to stray this far from the cottage, but the quiet of the night and the pull of her restless thoughts had drawn her onward. The world felt still, heavy with possibility, until she stumbled upon a secluded hut, its weathered planks barely visible through the haze.

She stopped, her heart picking up a nervous rhythm. Something about this place felt different—charged.

Compelled by a mix of curiosity and unease, she crept closer. A faint glow flickered from within, casting dancing shadows against the warped wood. Pressing herself against the hut's wall, she found a narrow gap between the planks and peeked inside.

A man stood at the center of the room, commanding her attention as if he belonged to an entirely different world. His hair shimmered in the dim light, framing sharp, striking features. His hands moved with practiced grace, tracing patterns in the air that left trails of shimmering energy in their wake.

Conivx's breath caught. She had never seen anything like this before.

The chill seeping through the cracks wrapped around her like an unspoken invitation. She shivered, not from fear, but from the strange pull of what unfolded before her.

The man's voice rose, his words carrying through the hut like a haunting melody.

"Nihil aeternum est praeter mortem."

A shiver crawled down Conivx's spine.

"Nothing is eternal except death," she translated, her brow furrowing. Then, a thought took root. *But what if... what if death itself could be conquered?*

The idea was intoxicating, a siren's call that threatened to dash her moral compass against the rocks of ambition. She leaned in closer, her breath fogging the wooden gap as she strained to hear every word.

Inside, the air rippled, bending and twisting as though reality itself was being rewritten.

Conivx's pulse quickened. She didn't know what he was doing, but it was magic—real magic. The kind she had only dreamed of wielding.

A familiar ache stirred within her, one she had carried all her life. She thought of Vespera—so beloved, so effortlessly admired. No matter what Conivx did, she was always second, always in the background.

But watching this man, watching the raw power flow through his veins, she felt something close to hope.

If she could learn magic like this, she wouldn't just matter—she would be *unstoppable*.

The man's voice pulled her from her thoughts, deep and resonant, sending another shiver down her spine. She had never seen him before, didn't even know his name, but he felt significant. Like a door left slightly ajar, leading to something greater.

She leaned in, heart pounding, as the ritual reached its climax. The air inside thickened, charged with an otherworldly energy that pressed against her skin, making her breath hitch.

She committed each movement, each syllable, to memory.

Then—*creak*.

The wooden deck beneath her feet betrayed her.

Conivx froze, her pulse hammering.

But the man remained lost in his ritual, his focus unwavering.

Slowly, she exhaled, relief washing over her. She had come too close to ruin, too close to losing everything.

With one last lingering glance at the man's shadowed form, she melted back into the mist, her mind alive with dark possibilities and her heart heavy with the weight of her ambition.

3

Conivx lingered in the shadows of the village square, her gaze fixed on Vespera.

Her sister's laughter rang out, warm and effortless, drawing people to her like moths to a flame. Vespera's golden-brown hair caught the sunlight as she embraced an elderly woman, her kindness so palpable it made Conivx's teeth clench.

"Oh, you're too kind," Vespera gushed, accepting a bouquet of wildflowers from a young girl. "These are beautiful. Thank you."

Conivx's lips curled into a sneer. How easily Vespera won them over, while she remained an outsider. The sting of rejection settled in her chest—a familiar ache, one she had carried for as long as she could remember.

Steeling herself, she stepped out of the shadows and forced a smile.

"Good day," she said, approaching a group of women chatting by the well. "Mind if I join you?"

The conversation died instantly. The women exchanged

quick glances, their smiles stiff. One of them, a plump matron with graying hair, hesitated before clearing her throat.

"Of course. Did you need something?"

Conivx's smile tightened.

"Not at all," she said smoothly. "Just looking for some pleasant company. Anything interesting happening with the harvest?"

"It's going well enough," another woman replied, her tone polite but clipped. "Though I doubt that's something you'd be concerned with."

Conivx's fingers twitched.

"On the contrary," she said lightly. "I find all aspects of village life fascinating. Maybe you could show me your gardens sometime?"

The women murmured vague, noncommittal responses, but their attention was already drifting—toward Vespera.

Conivx followed their gazes, watching as her sister moved effortlessly through the square, leaving smiles in her wake. Vespera didn't have to try—people simply gravitated toward her, drawn in by the warmth of her laughter, the effortless grace of her steps. They saw her kindness and sunshine, a beacon in their otherwise simple lives. And Conivx? She was the shadow that trailed behind.

The frustration burned, sharp and hot. She turned back to the women, pushing forward before they could brush her aside.

"I actually know quite a bit about herbs," she said, forcing her tone to stay light. "Maybe I could help—"

"That's kind of you," the matron interrupted, her smile thin, "but we've got it handled." She gave a quick nod before turning away. "Come on, ladies, lots to do."

And just like that, they left, their skirts swishing as they hurried off.

Conivx stood frozen by the well, her grip tightening around

the stone edge until her knuckles turned white. She tried to smile the way Vespera did—once, years ago. It had earned her nothing but wary glances, as if her smile concealed some hidden cruelty. Her guarded nature, born from years of rejection, had become their proof of her coldness.

Her sister didn't even have to try, and they adored her. But Conivx? She would always be the one they whispered about. The one left standing in the shadows. The one they feared without ever giving her a chance to prove them wrong.

And, gods help her, she was tired of standing there.

The village square fell silent.

Laughter and chatter died away as a tall, imposing figure moved through the crowd, his steps measured, unhurried. His flowing robes—deep indigo and black—whispered against the cobblestones, the arcane symbols embroidered along the fabric seeming to shift in the fading light.

Conivx's breath hitched. She shrank deeper into the shadows, eyes locked on him.

Him.

The man she had watched in secret all those weeks ago. The one who had bent reality itself with nothing but his voice and will.

The villagers parted before him like water before a great ship, their expressions a mix of awe and quiet reverence.

"Lord Kaeltharion," an elderly man stammered, bowing low. "An honor, as always."

Kaeltharion's lips curved into an easy smile, but his piercing gold eyes held no warmth. "The honor is mine. Everything is well, I trust?"

His voice was rich, smooth—like silk over steel. The kind of voice that could command a room without effort.

A young woman stepped forward, her eyes alight with admiration. "The miscreants haven't dared come near since you arrived. We can finally sleep at night because of you."

Kaeltharion inclined his head, gracious but unreadable. "It is my duty to protect you."

He moved through the square, pausing to clasp a shoulder, to murmur a reassuring word. The villagers hung on his every gesture, his every breath.

And Conivx couldn't look away.

There was something about him—something magnetic.

Power clung to him like a second skin, humming just beneath the surface, crackling in the air around him. He carried himself with quiet control, like he knew exactly how much he was capable of.

She inched closer, straining to hear more.

"They say he can raise the dead," someone whispered nearby.

"Or command the shadows themselves," another added.

Conivx's pulse quickened.

Power like that... The very idea of it made her chest tighten, her thoughts swirl.

She had spent her whole life living in the dim glow of her sister's light. Watching Vespera be adored, trusted—*chosen*. But this? This was something different.

She wasn't sure if it was admiration, envy, or something else entirely, but she felt *drawn* to him.

I must know more.

A plan was already forming in her mind, quick as wildfire.

Whatever secrets Kaeltharion held, she would uncover them. And when she did—when she learned what made him so powerful—Vespera wouldn't shine so brightly anymore.

As Kaeltharion turned to leave, his piercing gold eyes locked onto Conivx's brown ones. For a heartbeat, the world seemed to still. Then, his lips curled into a knowing smile, an unspoken acknowledgment passing between them.

Conivx's breath caught in her throat. That smile... it held secrets, promises, and something darker that made her skin prickle with anticipation. She inclined her head slightly, returning his smile with one of her own, equally enigmatic.

He knows, she thought, her pulse quickening.

Without a word, Kaeltharion turned and strode away, his dark robes billowing behind him. Conivx hesitated for only a moment before following, her steps silent as a cat's.

She melted into the shadows, her heart pounding with a mixture of excitement and trepidation. The village streets grew quieter as she trailed Kaeltharion, the cobblestones giving way to packed earth. The scent of pine and night-blooming jasmine filled the air, intoxicating in its intensity.

What game are you playing, Kaeltharion? Conivx wondered, her senses alert for any sign of danger. *And more importantly, how can I turn it to my advantage?*

She paused at the edge of a small clearing, hidden behind an ancient oak. Kaeltharion stood in the center, bathed in moonlight, his staff planted firmly in the ground. The air crackled with untapped power, making the hairs on the back of Conivx's neck stand on end.

Conivx's eyes widened as Kaeltharion began to chant, his voice a deep, resonant thrum that seemed to vibrate through the very earth. The obsidian staff in his grip pulsed, veins of eerie gold light slithering across its surface, as if the weapon itself were alive.

Then, the ground trembled.

Dark tendrils of energy spiraled from his staff, twisting and writhing like living shadows, slithering across the clearing with a hunger that sent a shiver up Conivx's spine. The moonlight dimmed, as if retreating from the raw power that now filled the air.

By the gods, Conivx thought, her breath catching in her throat. *Such power... such terrible, beautiful power.*

Then, the earth split apart.

The soil ruptured as skeletal hands clawed their way free, their brittle fingers stretching toward the sky. Mist coiled around the shifting ground, rising like smoke as dozens of corpses pulled themselves from the abyss of death. Fleshless skulls gleamed in the fractured moonlight, their empty sockets glowing with an unnatural sickly yellow light.

He was raising the dead.

Not as mindless husks. Not as mindless warriors. But as his sentinels, his guardians, his will manifest in bone and shadow.

The specters and reanimated corpses stood in perfect, unnatural silence. Kaeltharion gestured sharply, and in eerie synchronization, the risen dead turned toward the village that lay beyond the tree line.

"You will watch over them," Kaeltharion intoned, his voice layered with an ancient authority that made even the night tremble. "Guard them until dawn. Let no harm come to them."

The skeletal soldiers bowed in perfect, unnatural unison, their bony frames clicking and shifting as they silently obeyed.

She watched, transfixed, consumed by the sheer magnitude of what she was witnessing.

A war raged within her.

Fear clawed at her heart, whispering of the dangers of dark magic, of the price it demanded. But beneath that fear, a fierce hunger bloomed.

Knowledge. Power. The ability to shape reality itself.

This is what I've been searching for, Conivx realized, her fingers curling into fists at her sides. *This is how I'll finally step out of Vespera's shadow.*

Before she could second-guess herself, Conivx stepped out

from behind the oak tree. Her heart thundered in her chest, but her voice was steady as she called out,

"Teach me."

Kaeltharion's chanting ceased abruptly. The swirling energy dissipated, and the last of the sentinels vanished into the trees, melting into the night like living shadows. Only the moonlight remained, along with the weight of unspoken possibilities hanging in the air between them.

He turned.

His golden eyes, glowing faintly in the dim light, bore into her with an intensity that both thrilled and terrified her.

"You play a dangerous game, little sorceress," he murmured, his voice low and rich with promise.

Conivx lifted her chin, meeting his gaze unflinchingly.

"I'm well aware of the risks," she replied. "The question is, are you willing to take one on me?"

Kaeltharion's lips curled into a slow, knowing smile, his teeth catching the moonlight in a way that made them seem just a little too sharp.

"Bold," he murmured, stepping toward her. "I have to say, I admire someone who not only spies on me once but twice and still has the audacity to ask for my time. But tell me, Conivx Alderan—why should I entertain your request?"

Conivx's dark eyes flashed, bitterness coiling inside her like a snake. "My sister and I were once noble Ladies of Aurian," she said, her voice steady, but laced with something sharp. "We were cast out—left to the mercy of the sea like discarded scraps."

She could still hear it—the crash of waves, the splintering wood, the desperate struggle against an unforgiving tide.

"We washed up here with nothing but our names and the clothes on our backs," she continued, her tone hardening. "And yet, somehow, Vespera thrives. The villagers love her, while I…" She exhaled sharply. "I remain an outcast."

Kaeltharion tilted his head slightly, studying her. "The burden of living in someone else's shadow can be… *crushing*."

Conivx's gaze snapped to his, searching for any hint of mockery. She found none.

"They exiled me for wanting more," she said, her voice quieter now but no less firm. "For daring to seek magic and power beyond their narrow-minded rules."

She clenched her fists, but it was the next words that tightened her throat. "Vespera took part of the blame. They cast her out too. They were afraid of what I might become."

The admission was bitter. Her older sister, the one they had loved so much, had suffered because of her. But Vespera had *chosen* to share her fate, whether out of love or guilt, and Conivx could never decide which was worse.

Kaeltharion chuckled, low and dark. "And what exactly might that be?"

Conivx held his gaze, her next words barely above a whisper. "Someone like you."

A flicker of something passed through his expression—amusement, intrigue. She had his attention now.

The air between them thickened, charged with an energy she didn't quite understand yet. Then, with a slow wave of his hand, Kaeltharion's form shimmered. His flesh seemed to melt away, revealing glimpses of bone and something other beneath—an eerie, ghostlike energy that pulsed and flickered.

Conivx sucked in a breath.

"You're a lich," she murmured, equal parts awe and disbelief.

Kaeltharion's form shifted back as easily as if he'd simply changed his coat. "Indeed," he said smoothly. He gestured around them. "I keep this village safe from the creatures that roam this isle. And in return, they give me… community."

Conivx's mind raced. "They worship you."

His lips twitched. "A strong word. But they do respect me, which is more than most can say."

She stepped closer. "Teach me."

Kaeltharion arched a brow. "Oh?"

"You already see potential in me," she pressed, holding his gaze. "The same darkness that flows through you—it calls to me, too. I don't fear it. I want to understand it."

Kaeltharion circled her now, slow, deliberate. "And what about your sister?" he mused. "Sweet Vespera, beloved by all. Would you turn your back on her so easily?"

Bitterness twisted in Conivx's chest. Her jaw tightened.

"Vespera," she spat, the name tasting like ash. "Always Vespera."

Memories crashed over her—the whispers at court, the sideways glances. *The Alderan sisters. One so bright, the other... well.* The shipwreck, the endless fight for survival, and through it all, Vespera had *shone*. Always drawing people in, always leaving Conivx in the shadows.

But she had learned to live in the shadows. To thrive in them.

"She's not who they think she is," Conivx said quietly, turning back to Kaeltharion. "None of them are. But you... You see the truth, don't you? The power in embracing what others fear."

His golden eyes gleamed with interest. "Perhaps," he mused. "But tell me, what would you do with such power, Conivx Alderan?"

Her fingers twitched at her side, as if reaching for a sword that didn't yet exist.

"I would reshape the world," she whispered. "Starting with the people who cast us aside."

Kaeltharion's smile was slow, dangerous, full of something

dark and knowing. He stepped closer, his presence wrapping around Conivx like a shadow, like something inescapable.

"Such ambition," he murmured, his breath ghosting over her cheek. "It's… intoxicating."

Conivx's heart pounded, a heady mix of exhilaration and something deeper, something almost primal. She met his gaze, refusing to back down.

"Then teach me," she whispered. "Show me the power others are too afraid to claim."

His hand lifted, fingers tracing the air just inches from her skin. The air between them crackled, magic—dark, seductive— whispering over her like a promise.

"The price is steep," Kaeltharion warned, his voice rough, low. "Are you willing to pay it?"

Conivx barely hesitated. "I've already paid in blood and exile," she said, tilting her chin up. "What's a little more?"

A dark chuckle, rich and sinful, rumbled in his chest.

Finally, his fingers brushed her cheek, featherlight at first, then firmer, his touch cool yet searing. Conivx inhaled sharply, the sensation sending heat curling through her.

"Oh, my dear," Kaeltharion purred, his thumb tracing the curve of her jaw, lingering just beneath her lips. "We are going to do *such* great and terrible things together."

Her lashes fluttered, a slow breath escaping her. He felt like a force of nature, something impossible to resist. And she didn't *want* to resist.

She parted her lips, just slightly. "When do we begin?"

Kaeltharion's thumb dragged over her lower lip, the touch almost teasing, almost possessive. His gaze burned into hers, something wicked sparking in his golden eyes.

"We already have."

4

———————

Shadows danced along the walls as Conivx lifted her trembling hands, dark energy crackling between her fingertips. The room pulsed with raw magic, the air charged with something electric, something alive. It sent a shiver racing over her skin, making her breath hitch.

She had been training with Kaeltharion for weeks, pushing herself past every limit. And now, she could feel it—power, potent and waiting, ready to be shaped.

"Focus," Kaeltharion murmured from behind her, his voice like silk and smoke. His breath was cool against her neck, his presence impossibly close. "Feel the darkness inside you. Let it flow."

Conivx inhaled sharply, reaching deep within herself. The power surged, intoxicating and terrifying all at once. The candles in the room flickered wildly—then died, plunging them into near-total darkness.

"Yes," Kaeltharion hissed approvingly. "Now shape it. Bend it to your will."

She flicked her wrist, and the shadows obeyed, writhing

across the floor, twisting into monstrous forms. They snarled and snapped, reflections of something untamed within her.

A slow chuckle rumbled from Kaeltharion's chest as he circled her like a predator. "Impressive," he murmured. "You take to this as if you were born for it."

A thrill shot through her at his praise. "It feels... incredible," she admitted, watching the darkness move at her command. She turned her head slightly, just enough to glimpse him out of the corner of her eye. "Is this how you feel all the time?"

Kaeltharion's smile was a razor's edge. "This is but a taste, Conivx," he murmured, his voice rich with promise. "There are depths of power you've yet to even imagine."

She swallowed, her pulse thrumming.

As the lesson continued, she found herself watching him. The way his silver hair caught the faint light, how his hands moved so effortlessly, commanding forces she barely understood. She told herself it was admiration. But deep down, she knew it was more.

"You're distracted," Kaeltharion observed, his golden eyes piercing through her.

Conivx felt heat rise to her cheeks. "I... I'm sorry," she said quickly, but her voice betrayed her. "It's just—the way you wield magic, the control you have... it's mesmerizing."

A slow, knowing smile curved his lips. "Power can be intoxicating," he said smoothly, stepping closer, "but remember—it always demands a price."

Conivx held his gaze, unflinching. "I've already lost everything," she murmured. "I'll pay whatever it takes."

Kaeltharion's eyes darkened, something dangerous flickering in their depths.

"You truly mean that," he mused, studying her.

Conivx leaned in slightly, her voice dropping to a silken whisper. "Tell me," she purred, tilting her head just enough to let her hair fall over one shoulder. "What's the hardest part of your craft? Surely someone like you has overcome every obstacle."

Her fingers absently toyed with her obsidian bracelet—a subtle, deliberate movement designed to draw his attention. His gaze flickered down, a ghost of amusement touching his lips.

"The greatest challenge," he said, his voice low, "is not in raising the dead—but in controlling them. To bend a soul to your will requires more than power. It takes... command."

Conivx's breath hitched.

Control. That was the key.

"And how does one master such a thing?" she asked, leaning just a fraction closer. The scent of night-blooming jasmine clung to her skin, curling around them both.

Kaeltharion's gaze met hers, and for a moment—just a moment—something flickered behind those piercing golden eyes. Was it intrigue? Affection? Something deeper?

He reached out, tucking a stray lock of raven hair behind her ear. His touch was surprisingly gentle, lingering just long enough to make her chest tighten.

"It takes years," he murmured, his fingers ghosting over her cheek. "And the willingness to sacrifice everything."

Her heart pounded against her ribs. This unexpected tenderness—was it a test? A manipulation? Or something real?

She forced herself to stay still, to hold his gaze, even as every instinct screamed at her to step back. Instead, she let her lips part slightly, a calculated mix of innocence and challenge.

"I am willing," she whispered. "To learn. To sacrifice. To become more."

Kaeltharion's expression shifted, something unreadable flashing through his eyes.

Had she just ensnared him? Or had he ensnared her?

They settled by the fire, the flickering flames casting long, twisting shadows across his face. He was watching her, and for the first time, she wasn't sure who had the upper hand.

"There are... forces at work on this island," he said at last, his voice low, thoughtful. "Ancient powers, far older than the magic you now wield. Even I must tread carefully."

Conivx leaned forward, her curiosity ignited. "What kind of powers?"

Kaeltharion's gaze grew distant, lost in some long-buried memory. "Long ago, I made a bargain," he said finally. "It granted me knowledge, power… but at a terrible cost."

Her pulse quickened. "What was the cost?"

His golden eyes met hers, filled with something she had never seen before.

"My humanity."

The firelight flickered, casting eerie shadows along the walls. Conivx hesitated, then slowly, almost hesitantly, let her fingers brush against his hand. A silent question. A wordless plea.

"You were mortal?" she whispered.

Kaeltharion's gaze didn't waver. "Once." His lips quirked slightly, but the expression held no warmth. "I was as fleeting as the villagers you so easily dismiss."

Her heart pounded. "What happened?"

He hesitated. Then, after a long moment, his fingers curled around hers—light at first, but unmistakably possessive.

"Desperation," he admitted. "Ambition. A thirst for knowledge that could not be sated. I wanted freedom—from mortality, from the chains of time itself."

She exhaled slowly. "And you found it."

"I did," he said, but there was something bitter in his tone.

His thumb brushed over her knuckles absently, as if lost in thought. "Deep in the heart of this cursed isle lies something ancient. A being of shadow and malice. I made a pact with it, and in return…" His lips pressed into a thin line. "It took everything."

Conivx shivered. "And yet… you would still do it again."

Kaeltharion's smile was slow, knowing. "Wouldn't you?"

She didn't answer. She didn't have to.

He leaned closer, the air between them humming with something unspoken. "Be careful, Conivx," he murmured, his voice barely audible. "Power will consume you, piece by piece, until there's nothing left."

Conivx tilted her chin up, her lips curling into a faint, defiant smile. "Then let it."

Kaeltharion's fingers lingered at her jaw, his gaze searching hers, dark and unreadable. For a moment, they simply stood there, suspended in the tension between warning and desire.

Then, so softly it was almost imperceptible, he whispered—

"It already has."

5

The moon hung low, casting a ghostly glow over the village rooftops. Conivx stood barefoot on the cool stone path outside their cottage, her arms crossed tightly over her chest as she watched the trees sway in the distance. She had just returned from another late-night session with Kaeltharion, her muscles aching and her thoughts in disarray.

The front door creaked open behind her.

"You're home late," Vespera's voice drifted out, soft but edged with something unreadable.

Conivx didn't turn. "He wanted to push my limits. Said I needed to learn control." Her tone was neutral, but her fingers tightened around her elbows.

Vespera stepped outside, pulling a shawl tightly around her shoulders. Her golden-brown hair shimmered in the moonlight, the strands catching the breeze like gossamer threads. "You've been spending a lot of time with him lately."

Conivx arched a brow, still staring out at the dark horizon. "He's my mentor. Isn't that what I'm supposed to do?"

Vespera hesitated, then took a step closer. "Yes, but... maybe it's time to give yourself a break. Rest. You've been looking worn out lately." She offered a small smile, but it didn't reach her eyes.

Conivx finally turned to face her sister. "You think I'm weak."

"No," Vespera said quickly. "That's not what I meant."

"Then what *do* you mean?" The words came out sharper than she intended, laced with something brittle and defensive. "Because lately, it feels like you don't want me training with him at all."

Vespera's hands fidgeted with the edge of her shawl. "It's not that. I just worry about you. Kaeltharion has his own goals. He doesn't always consider—"

"I'm not some helpless girl in need of protection." Conivx took a step forward, her voice gaining heat. "I *need* this. I'm getting stronger. Strong enough to—"

"To what?" Vespera interrupted, her voice tight. "To prove something to him? Or to yourself?"

The silence that followed was deafening.

Conivx stared at her, her jaw clenched. "What are you trying to say?"

Vespera's gaze faltered, guilt flickering in her amber eyes. "Nothing. I just… don't want you to get hurt."

Conivx's laugh was short and humorless. "Too late for that."

Vespera's expression twisted, as if the words cut deeper than they should have. "Conivx, I'm trying to help—"

"No, you're trying to *steer* me. Away from him. Why?" Conivx's eyes narrowed. "You've never cared about my training before. What changed?"

Vespera hesitated for one breath too long. "I just think… maybe you're putting your trust in the wrong person."

"And who should I trust, then?" Conivx asked, stepping closer now, her voice low and dangerous. "You?"

Vespera didn't answer.

Something unreadable passed between them. A chasm widening.

Conivx shook her head slowly. "You've been keeping things from me."

"I'm not," Vespera said too quickly.

"You're lying," Conivx whispered, her voice suddenly hollow.

Vespera reached out, placing a hand on Conivx's arm. "Please, just—be careful. That's all I'm asking."

Conivx pulled away. "I don't need your concern. I need the truth."

Vespera's lips parted, but no words came.

Without another glance, Conivx turned and walked into the house, the door slamming shut behind her.

6

Eonivx stood near the window, her slender frame outlined by the silvery glow of the moon. The past few months had changed her—softness giving way to something sharper, something untamed. Her long black hair tumbled down her back like a veil of midnight, a striking contrast against her pale skin.

In her hands, she held an open tome, its pages brimming with arcane symbols that pulsed faintly with magic. She traced one with her fingertips, feeling the energy hum beneath her touch.

"You're distracted again," Kaeltharion's voice came from behind her, smooth and deep, like a blade wrapped in silk.

She didn't turn, only let out a slow breath. "And you're late." A smirk ghosted across her lips. "I was beginning to think you'd lost your nerve. Or worse—your interest."

Kaeltharion chuckled as he leaned against the doorframe, arms crossed over his broad chest. "Interest? In you?" His voice dropped as he pushed off the frame and strode toward her with the effortless grace of a predator. "Oh, Conivx, you are far too intriguing to ignore."

She finally turned to face him, meeting his golden eyes with a knowing look. "Flattery will get you nowhere," she said, though there was a challenge in her gaze.

"Who says I'm flattering you?" He stopped just inches away, his presence wrapping around her like a lingering spell. "Besides, I'd argue I've already taught you plenty."

"Not enough," she countered, stepping closer, refusing to look away. "I want more—more power, more knowledge. You said you could give it to me. Was that a lie?"

For the briefest moment, his smile faltered. Then he reached out, brushing a strand of her hair back, his fingers lingering against her cheek.

"You have potential," he murmured. "But power isn't something I can simply hand to you. It has to be earned."

Her breath came a little quicker, but she refused to let him see the effect he had on her. "And I'm willing to earn it," she said. "But you're holding back. I can feel it. You don't trust me."

His eyes darkened. "Trust isn't given lightly, not in our world." His thumb traced the curve of her jaw, the gesture almost affectionate. "And you—you're dangerous, Conivx. Ambitious. Clever. Ruthless when you need to be. That's why I chose you. But it's also why I'm cautious."

Her lips parted, caught between the weight of his words and the heat of his touch. Then her chin lifted, defiant. "You're afraid of me."

Kaeltharion laughed, low and rich. "Afraid? No, little sorceress. I'm intrigued by you. And that makes you dangerous to me."

The air between them thickened, charged with something neither of them would name. He was close enough that she could see the way his pupils dilated, how his fingers twitched like he was holding himself back.

She stepped closer, closing the space between them until their bodies nearly touched. She tilted her head up, her breath warm against his lips. "Then stop holding back," she whispered. "Show me what you're so afraid of."

Kaeltharion's hand slid to the back of her neck, his fingers threading through her hair as his grip tightened just enough to make her pulse stutter. His golden eyes burned, his control fraying at the edges.

"Careful what you wish for," he murmured before his lips crushed against hers.

The moment they touched, everything else melted away.

His kiss was demanding, consuming, like fire and darkness colliding. His hands roamed her back, pulling her against him as her fingers tangled in his hair, her nails dragging along his scalp. A quiet groan rumbled in his chest as he deepened the kiss, pressing her against the cool stone wall.

Conivx had imagined power in many forms—raw magic, dark knowledge, bending shadows to her will. But this? This was power too, the kind that curled around her ribs and sent heat pooling low in her stomach.

She wasn't sure who was claiming who.

Their movements were urgent, almost desperate, as if they were both trying to take control, to prove something neither could quite put into words. His lips left hers only to trail along her jaw, down the column of her throat. Her breath hitched, her hands fisting in his robes.

Even as she melted into him, her mind whispered one undeniable truth.

This was dangerous.

Not just the magic, not just their ambitions. This. *Him.*

She was playing with fire, but she wasn't sure she wanted to put it out.

Kaeltharion finally pulled away, both of them breathing

hard. His eyes searched hers, something flickering behind the gold—something she almost mistook for hesitation.

"You're playing a dangerous game, Conivx," he said, his voice lower now, rougher.

She let out a slow breath, her lips still tingling. "So are you," she murmured, steady despite the pounding of her heart. "But I'm not afraid to lose. Are you?"

For a moment, she thought he might kiss her again. Instead, he stepped back, his expression once again unreadable.

"Our lessons aren't over," he said briskly, as if nothing had happened. "But you'll need more than raw talent and determination to succeed."

She arched a brow, lips still curved from the ghost of his kiss. "And you'll need more than charm to keep me in check."

He chuckled, shaking his head. "I think I've created a monster."

"Not yet," she said, turning back to the window. "But soon."

She heard the door click shut behind him.

Still, she didn't move. Her pulse was too loud in her ears, her thoughts too tangled. She had tasted his power, his passion, and she wanted more. But she also sensed that he was hiding something, something he wasn't ready to share.

And that only made her more determined to uncover his secrets—no matter what it cost.

7

The shadows lengthened as Conivx crept through the village, her heart a thunderous drumbeat in her chest. Ahead, Kaeltharion's silver hair gleamed in the twilight, a beacon she followed with desperate intensity. Her eyes narrowed as he glanced furtively over his shoulder, unaware of her presence.

"Where are you going?" she whispered, her words carried away by the chill wind that swept through the deserted streets.

Kaeltharion's path led him to the outskirts of the village, where dilapidated cottages gave way to twisted trees. Conivx pressed herself against rough bark, her breath catching as Kaeltharion paused in a small clearing.

"You came," a familiar voice rang out, and Conivx's blood turned to ice.

Vespera emerged from the shadows, her golden-brown hair cascading over her shoulders. Kaeltharion's face softened, his usual mask of arrogance melting away.

"Always," he murmured, pulling Vespera close.

Conivx's world shattered as their lips met. The kiss was

tender, intimate – everything she had longed for. Her nails dug into the tree bark, splinters embedding themselves in her flesh as she struggled to comprehend the betrayal unfolding before her.

How long? she thought, her mind reeling. *How long have they been deceiving me?*

Kaeltharion's hands traced the curve of Vespera's face with a gentleness Conivx had never witnessed. "My love," he whispered, the endearment a dagger to Conivx's heart.

Vespera's amber eyes shone with adoration. "I've missed you," she breathed.

Conivx's vision blurred, tears threatening to spill over. She wanted to scream, to unleash her fury upon them both. But she remained frozen, a silent witness to her own undoing.

"We must be careful," Kaeltharion cautioned, his voice low. "If Conivx were to discover—"

"She won't," Vespera assured him, her fingers entwining with his. "I know my sister. She sees only what she wants to see."

The words struck Conivx like a physical blow. Had she truly been so blind? So easily manipulated?

As Kaeltharion and Vespera melted into the shadows once more, their whispered endearments fading into the night, Conivx remained motionless. The weight of their betrayal crushed her, each breath a struggle against the tide of anguish threatening to drown her.

Conivx's world shattered, each fragment a reflection of her broken dreams. Her dark eyes, once filled with ambition, now burned with the intensity of a thousand dying stars. She staggered backward, her usually graceful movements now clumsy and desperate.

"No," she whispered, her voice raw with anguish. "It can't be..."

But the truth was undeniable. The swell of Vespera's belly,

barely visible beneath her flowing gown, mocked Conivx's ignorance. How had she not made sense of it before now?

Her mind raced, piecing together fragments of memories. Vespera's secretive smiles, her evasive answers about the child's father. It all made sense now, a cruel joke at her expense.

Conivx's fingers clawed at the rough bark of a nearby tree, seeking any anchor in this storm of betrayal. "I trusted you," she hissed, her words lost to the uncaring night. "Both of you."

She stumbled away from the scene, each step heavy with the weight of her shattered illusions. The isle, once a realm of possibility, now seemed to close in around her, its shadows reaching out with grasping tendrils.

I was a fool, Conivx thought, her internal voice dripping with self-loathing. *Blinded by my own ambition, by my... feelings for him.*

As she retreated, the sounds of the night seemed to mock her. The rustle of leaves became Kaeltharion's whispered endearments, the distant howl of a wolf transformed into Vespera's laughter.

Conivx's retreat became a frantic flight, her feet carrying her through the twisted paths of the isle. She fled not just from the scene of betrayal, but from the remnants of her former self.

8

———

Conivx's feet pounded against the damp earth, her breath coming in ragged gasps. The mist-shrouded forest stretched endlessly before her, its twisted trees looming like silent sentinels. Behind her, the village—her home, her prison—disappeared into the fog, swallowed by shadows that reached for her like spectral fingers.

Her lungs burned, but the pain was nothing compared to the inferno in her chest.

Betrayal.

The word echoed in her mind with every frantic heartbeat, twisting through her like poison.

"How could they?" she rasped, each word dripping with anger. "My own sister. My mentor."

Images seared her thoughts—Vespera's golden-brown hair tangled in Kaeltharion's fingers, their lips pressed together in a passionate embrace. The sight had burned itself into her soul, scorching away the last remnants of trust she had left.

Her knees hit the forest floor. She barely felt the impact. Her fingers curled into the damp soil, digging in as though she could tear her pain straight from the earth.

"I trusted them," she whispered, her voice hollow. "I loved them."

But love, she realized, was a weakness. A tool for the cunning to manipulate the foolish. And she had been *so* foolish.

Conivx lifted her head, her dark eyes gleaming with something new—something sharp, cold, and unstoppable.

"No more."

The mist thickened around her, coiling at her feet like a living thing, as if it had heard her vow and answered in kind.

"Oh, sister dear," she murmured, her lips curling into a mirthless smile. "Did you really think I would fade away? That I would accept your betrayal like some helpless child?"

She laughed then, a sound that sent unseen creatures scurrying into the underbrush.

"And Kaeltharion," she continued, rolling his name over her tongue like venom. "My dear, dear mentor. You taught me well. Perhaps too well."

She pushed herself to her feet, her body steady, her resolve solidifying with every breath.

"You both sought to keep me in the shadows," she snarled. "To deny me my rightful power. But the darkness is not something to be feared. It is meant to be embraced."

The mist surged around her, swallowing the last vestiges of warmth from the air. Conivx closed her eyes, feeling it—something ancient brushing against her mind, a whisper of something far greater than herself.

"I am coming for you," she whispered, a promise and a warning. "And when I do, you will learn what true fear is."

Then she turned and walked deeper into the forest, her steps slow, deliberate. Behind her, the mist closed in, erasing her footprints, carrying away the echo of her laughter—a sound that would haunt the nightmares of those who had wronged her.

Her pace slowed as she stumbled into a clearing, the air suddenly still.

It felt different here.

Heavy. Charged with something unseen. The hairs on the back of her neck prickled.

Conivx hesitated, her breath shallow. "What is this place?"

A whisper drifted through the trees, curling around her ears like smoke.

Conivx... Come closer...

She took a step forward, her pulse hammering. "Who's there?"

Deeper... Come deeper into the shadows...

Something inside her screamed to turn back. But another part—the part that craved power, that burned with rage—urged her forward.

Her feet moved on their own, drawn to the heart of the clearing. Every step sent a ripple through the ground beneath her, as though the very earth was alive, shifting in anticipation.

She forced herself to speak, her voice steadier than she felt. "I'm not afraid of you."

The darkness stirred.

A laugh—low, chilling—echoed all around her.

I have been waiting for you, Conivx Alderan.

The voice wasn't coming from one place. It was everywhere, a chorus of whispers that slithered into her mind.

Conivx turned sharply, searching the shadows. "What are you?"

Another laugh, deeper this time. *I am the ancient darkness. The power you have always craved.*

Her heart slammed against her ribs. "How do you know what I want?"

I know everything about you. Your desires. Your fears. Your need for vengeance.

The air around her thickened, pressing against her skin like invisible hands. The darkness curled at her feet, no longer just mist but something alive.

Her breath came in quick, uneven bursts. She could feel it. The power. The promise. The pull of something greater than anything she had ever known.

"And what do you want from me?" she whispered.

The shadows began to take form, condensing into a towering figure. Its body was shifting darkness, its eyes twin embers of violet light, burning with something ancient and knowing.

I offer you a choice, Conivx Alderan.

The voice rumbled through her bones.

Embrace me, and claim the power you have always desired.

The shadows pulsed around her, beckoning.

Or flee, and remain forever in your sister's shadow.

Conivx's hands clenched into fists.

There was no choice.

There had never been.

Conivx took a slow, deliberate breath, her decision solidifying like iron in her mind.

"I accept," she said, her voice steady despite the storm of emotions raging inside her. "Grant me the power to shape my own destiny."

The darkness surged forward.

It swallowed her whole.

A cold unlike anything she had ever known sank into her bones, wrapping around her like an iron vice. She gasped, her breath stolen by the sheer force of it. The air turned thick, heavy, pressing against her chest as if the very night sought to crush her.

Then came the pain.

It started as a slow burn beneath her skin, but quickly it escalated—searing, twisting agony tearing through every nerve. Her body convulsed, her limbs locking as the dark energy forced itself into every fiber of her being. She clawed at the earth, her nails digging deep, but there was no escaping it.

The shadows were inside her now.

"What... is happening to me?" she choked out, her voice barely more than a rasp.

You are becoming one with the darkness, the force whispered. *Embrace it.*

But it was not so simple.

Her veins burned as the essence of the isle itself coursed through her, raw and ancient. Her spine arched, a strangled scream escaping her lips as her body fought against the transformation. Her heartbeat pounded in her ears, erratic and frantic, before slowing, each beat heavier than the last.

Then—nothing.

Silence.

Darkness.

Days passed.

At first, she drifted in and out of consciousness, lost in a world of shifting shadows and whispering voices. Dreams and nightmares blurred together—visions of destruction, of vengeance, of a power beyond imagining. The pain dulled, but the ache remained, like the ghost of something torn from her and replaced with something... other.

When she finally opened her eyes, the world had changed.

Colors were sharper, more vivid, yet every shadow pulsed with an energy she could feel beneath her skin. Her body felt lighter, yet stronger, as if something had been unlocked within her.

She pushed herself upright, unsteady at first. A nearby pool of water reflected her new form, and she inhaled sharply.

Her once-dull brown eyes now burned with a luminous violet glow. Her raven hair rippled like living ink, shifting and curling in a nonexistent breeze. Pale, almost translucent skin revealed dark veins beneath the surface, pulsating with the magic now fused into her very being.

The sight should have unsettled her. Instead, she smiled.

"Is this the price of power?" she murmured, tracing the delicate lines of darkness that now marked her hands.

It is only the beginning, the voice answered, its tone laced with satisfaction. *Your humanity fades. Soon, you will be something far greater.*

Conivx exhaled, letting the truth settle over her like a comforting shroud.

"Good," she whispered. "Humanity is overrated."

She no longer flinched when the shadows moved at her will. They obeyed her now, bending to her thoughts before she could even voice a command. The forest, once a place of fear and uncertainty, now felt like an extension of herself. The mist coiled around her ankles like a faithful hound, awaiting orders.

She tested her power, summoning tendrils of darkness from the ground, twisting them into wicked shapes. With a flick of her wrist, she sent a sphere of pure shadow hurtling toward a tree. The impact was instant. The bark withered, cracked, and then—nothing. It had been reduced to dust.

A cold smile played across her lips.

"Oh, Kaeltharion," she purred. "You fool. You chose the wrong sister."

As she spoke his name, the rage surged again. She saw them, saw *him*—his lips on Vespera's, his hands tangled in her sister's golden hair.

She had trusted him.

She had loved him.

And in return, he had betrayed her.

With a furious snarl, she hurled another blast of energy, watching with grim satisfaction as another tree crumbled into nothing. The shadows around her pulsed, feeding off her fury, growing darker, stronger.

"I trusted you," she spat, her voice laced with venom. "Both of you. And for what? To be cast aside like I was nothing?"

She raised her hands, reveling in the raw power surging through her veins. The air itself trembled.

"Watch me, Vespera," she called out, her voice carrying unnaturally through the forest. "Watch as I tear down everything you hold dear. Your precious village. Your beloved Kaeltharion. All of it will burn."

Her laughter echoed through the trees, a sound both chilling and triumphant.

"And when I'm done," she whispered, "you'll finally understand. You'll see that I was always meant for greatness."

The wind howled in response, carrying her words like a promise—like a threat.

The shadows clung to her more tightly. She spent hours pacing the forest, lost in thoughts of vengeance, of power, of the destiny now laid before her.

Something was still missing.

A weapon.

She needed something to channel her strength, something worthy of the force she had become.

As if answering her call, the darkness at her feet coalesced, swirling and twisting, shaping itself to her will.

She extended her hand.

The shadows solidified into a blade, sleek and deadly, the metal darker than midnight, its edges lined with faint, pulsating violet veins. Jewels of the same color shimmered along its hilt, glowing softly, as if waiting for her touch.

She grasped it.

Power surged through her fingers, sealing the bond between them.

"Umbra," she whispered, naming the blade. "Together, we will carve a path of vengeance across this wretched isle."

She swung it once, testing the balance. Perfect.

A slow smile spread across her lips as she turned her gaze back toward the village, toward the people who had abandoned her.

"Oh, sister dear," she murmured into the wind, "I do hope you're prepared. The reckoning is coming."

She traced her fingers over the blade's edge, feeling the cold hum of magic beneath her touch.

"And it will be glorious."

9

———————

Conivx Alderan strode toward the village, her raven-black hair whipping behind her, her violet eyes burning with cold fury. Shadows clung to her like a living shroud, the air around her humming with dark energy that drained the warmth from the night itself. With every step, the ground trembled, as if the isle itself recoiled from what she had become.

The village remained unaware, blissfully ignorant of the storm about to consume them.

With a flick of her wrist, Conivx summoned flames—dark, hungry things that flickered at her fingertips, aching to be unleashed. She watched them curl and twist, savoring the power that surged through her veins.

They will all pay.

In one fluid motion, she hurled the shadow fire toward the village.

The flames roared to life, leaping from home to home, devouring wood and thatch with unnatural hunger. The peaceful night shattered into chaos—screams, the rush of panicked footsteps, the crackling of an unholy inferno. The sky glowed with sickly purple light, casting eerie, jagged shadows across the cobbled streets.

This is only the beginning.

Umbra was already in her grip, the dark blade thrumming with power. Her every movement was effortless, driven by an intoxicating force that made her feel untouchable.

At last, they will understand the price of betrayal.

She barely heard the screams, barely registered the faces twisted in terror. None of them mattered. Not anymore.

Then, through the smoke and destruction, a voice rang out— a voice she once knew better than her own.

"Sister, please! Stop this madness!"

Conivx turned.

Her older sister stood at the heart of the burning village, her amber eyes wide with horror, her hair wild in the wind and smoke. The fire behind her framed her like a figure from a dream, but the anguish on her face was all too real.

Conivx's expression darkened. "You dare stand against me?" she hissed, her voice like ice. "After everything I have suffered, you still cling to your pathetic notions of mercy?"

Vespera took a trembling step forward, hands outstretched in desperation. "Conivx, this isn't you. You're letting your pain destroy you. Please, let me help you—"

A cold, sharp laugh cut through the night.

"Help me?" Conivx sneered. "You think you can fix me? That I need saving?" She took a step closer, her blade low at her side, its edge glinting in the firelight. "No, sister. I am the one who was abandoned. I am the one who suffered while you lived in the light."

She is weak. She will never understand true power.

Vespera's voice broke. "This isn't who you are." Tears shimmered in her eyes, reflecting the destruction around them. "You were kind once. You loved our people. You loved me."

Conivx's grip tightened on Umbra, the blade pulsing in time with the rage pounding through her chest. "That girl is dead. She died the moment you turned your back on me. The moment you and Kaeltharion *betrayed* me."

Vespera's lips parted, her breath catching.

"You took everything from me," Conivx continued, her voice low and lethal. "The love of the village. The admiration of Kaeltharion. What could have been *my* child."

Vespera flinched, pain flashing across her face.

"I never meant—"

"Spare me your pity!" Conivx snarled. "You knew how I felt about him. And still, you took him for yourself. You had everything, and I was left with *nothing.*"

For a moment, silence stretched between them, thick with the weight of shattered trust. Then, with a feral cry, Conivx lunged.

Vespera barely moved in time. Umbra's blade cut across her back, leaving a jagged wound that sent her sprawling to the ground. A strangled cry escaped her lips as she clutched the dirt, struggling to rise.

"You'll never hurt me again," Conivx growled, raising Umbra for the final strike.

But before she could bring the blade down, a voice thundered through the chaos.

"Conivx, STOP!"

She froze.

Kaeltharion stepped from the shadows. His golden eyes blazed—not with fury, but with something far worse: Betrayal. Grief. Resolve. Power pulsed around him like a storm held barely in check.

Conivx turned slowly, her grip on Umbra tightening. "Come

to save her, have you?" she said, her voice dripping with venom. "How noble. How predictable."

Kaeltharion's gaze drifted to Vespera, who lay crumpled and wheezing in the dirt, her gown soaked in blood and ash. Then, he looked at Conivx—and something in him hardened.

"You've made a grave mistake," he said, voice low and shaking. "This pact with the darkness… I warned you what it did to me."

A cruel smile touched Conivx's lips. "You warned me because you were too weak to harness it. I'm not."

He took a step closer, face unreadable save for the quiet devastation in his eyes. "You never mattered to me the way she did."

The world stopped.

Conivx's breath caught in her throat. Her fingers loosened on the hilt for a heartbeat, her fury momentarily replaced by something dangerously fragile.

Then came the shattering.

"You *dare*?" she whispered, voice trembling—not with sorrow, but with fury so deep it tasted like blood.

Kaeltharion held her gaze, his expression unreadable, but his next words were deliberate, precise, meant to wound. "Vespera never had to beg for love. She didn't chase power to feel worthy. You could have conquered this entire isle and spent a thousand lifetimes chasing power, and it still wouldn't have been enough. Because no matter how hard you tried, deep down, you knew— no one ever chose you."

The silence that followed was short-lived.

A scream ripped from Conivx's throat, raw and ragged. Her hands surged with darkness, magic flaring wild and vicious. "You destroyed me long before I ever raised this blade!" she howled. "You made me *believe* I mattered."

"You mattered," Kaeltharion replied, "but only as a mirror of what I once was. Ambitious. Hungry. Dangerous. I loved the fire in you, Conivx. But all you ever wanted was power. Not love. Not peace."

"And now I have both," she snarled. "Power, *and* vengeance."

She raised her arms, summoning every ounce of corrupted magic that pulsed through her veins. "Let's see how your golden ideals hold up against oblivion."

The battle tore through the village, shadows clashing in violent bursts that split the sky. The ground trembled beneath their fury, the ruins of homes and lives reduced to smoldering embers. Conivx struck again and again, her magic a relentless storm fueled by rage and heartbreak. But Kaeltharion met her with equal force, his power unwavering, his golden eyes burning with something worse than anger—conviction.

"You were never meant to wield this power," Kaeltharion roared, countering her strike. "This darkness—it *feeds* on you. Just like it fed on me!" His necrotic energy clashed with her darkness, sending shockwaves through the earth.

"And yet, here I stand," Conivx spat, her voice raw. "Stronger than you ever were."

With a cry that tore through the sky, she slammed Umbra into the ground. Shadows surged from the blade, spiraling down into the earth like hungry serpents. The ground trembled, and with a sudden, violent crack, a chasm opened beneath Kaeltharion's feet.

He didn't scream as he fell. Instead, his voice rose with magic, ancient and damning.

"Conivx Alderan…"

The shadows around her stilled.

"By the blood you spilled, and the darkness you embraced, I bind you. As long as you live, so shall this isle. You will never leave it. You will never escape the consequences of your ambition."

Conivx's smirk faltered.

A curse.

Something deep and inescapable latched onto her soul, wrapping around her like chains. She gasped as the magic took hold, a force unlike anything she had ever known pulling at her very essence. The island breathed through her now, its will entwined with hers.

"You gave your soul to the dark, Conivx. And now, this isle is your prison. Your kingdom of ashes."

The chasm sealed behind him with a deafening rumble.

The wind howled through the ruins, the flames flickering in its wake. The sky darkened, as if the stars themselves mourned what had been done.

Conivx staggered, the weight of the spell pressing into her bones. She could feel the island now. It was inside her.

She would never leave.

She would never be free.

But she would *rule*.

A sharp cry split the silence.

Not a scream. Not the dying wails of the villagers.

A child.

Conivx turned, scanning the wreckage. Her eyes locked on a figure crumpled near the remnants of a charred wall. Vespera, holding the child, rocking him through her pain. Blood stained the back of her dress from the deep wound Umbra had left.

Slowly, Conivx approached.

"You should have run," Conivx said, voice low.

Vespera's eyes lifted to meet hers, glassy with pain. "I couldn't. He's my son."

"And you thought you could save him?" Conivx stood over her, the sword hanging at her side. "After everything you've taken from me?"

"I didn't take him from you," Vespera whispered. "Kaeltharion used us both. You just couldn't see it."

Conivx's jaw tightened. "He saw my power. He taught me what I needed to know. You stole his heart."

Vespera coughed, cradling the baby closer. "I didn't steal anything. He loved me. The way you always wanted to be loved."

The words struck like a blade to the chest. Conivx's fingers flexed around Umbra's hilt. "You always knew how to twist the knife. Even now."

"I never wanted to hurt you," Vespera said, tears streaking her ash-covered cheeks. "You were my sister."

"Sister." Conivx spat the word. "You were the light everyone adored. And me? The shadow you left behind."

Vespera's strength faltered, her body sagging as she held the baby up toward Conivx. "Please...not him. Let him live."

Conivx stared at the child. Innocent. Helpless. The last remnant of the sister who had overshadowed her entire life.

"He will live," Conivx said. "But not for you."

Vespera's eyes glistened with fresh tears. "We used to share everything, Con. Remember? When we were little and had no one but each other? Our parents... they would've been ashamed of this. Of us."

Conivx's grip on Umbra tightened. "They were ashamed of me long before tonight. I was always the strange one, the broken one. While you... you were their star."

"They loved you," Vespera whispered. "In their own way."

"If that were true, they never would have exiled me," Conivx corrected, voice sharp. "You were a fool to follow me here. Everything would have been perfect had you not *chosen* to be banished alongside me. All of this is your fault."

"It doesn't have to be this way," Vespera pleaded. "You can stop this. We can raise him together. Give him a different life."

A bitter laugh escaped Conivx. "Together?" Her eyes darkened. "No, Vespera. There is no 'we' anymore. You made sure of that when you took everything that was mine."

Vespera's breath faltered, her eyes closing briefly as the weight of those words sank in. "I forgive you," she whispered.

The words struck like ice through Conivx's chest. For a moment, she hesitated, the past—their childhood, their parents' voices, the warmth of simpler days—crashing into her like a wave.

But the island's power surged within her veins, feeding her rage, reminding her of the years she had been overlooked, unwanted.

"But I don't forgive you," Conivx said softly.

Umbra sliced through the air, piercing Vespera's chest. Her body arched, a strangled gasp escaping her lips before she collapsed.

The baby's cry rose in the stillness.

Conivx knelt and pried the child from her sister's lifeless arms. His wide, innocent eyes stared up at her, unaware of the monster that now held him.

Her breath was unsteady. The fury inside her should have burned hotter. She should have ended him, erased every trace of Vespera from the world.

But she didn't.

Instead, her grip tightened around the child, possessive.

"You are all that remains of my dear sister," she whispered. "And now, you belong to me."

The wind howled through the ruins, carrying away the last echoes of battle. The shadows curled at her feet, obedient and waiting.

With the child in her arms, Conivx stepped into the mist, disappearing into the darkness that had claimed her soul.

PART II

ANYA

10

———————

300 YEARS LATER

The storm raged like a beast unleashed, tearing through the night with furious winds and thunder that split the sky. Rain poured in heavy sheets, turning the forest into a shifting sea of silver and shadow.

Anya moved swiftly through the trees, her cloak soaked and heavy, her senses razor-sharp despite the downpour. Then—

A cry. Raw. Agonized.

She froze, heart hammering. It wasn't an animal. It was something else. Something *wrong*.

Another groan followed, weaker this time. Every instinct screamed for her to turn back, to return to the coven's protective wards. But she didn't. She couldn't.

Drawn by something she couldn't explain, she pressed forward, weaving through the tangled underbrush until she stumbled into a clearing.

And there, sprawled across the muddied ground like a fallen star, was a man.

No—*what had once been* a man.

His tunic, or what little remained, clung to his rain-soaked skin, streaked with blood and soot. His wings—massive, blackened things—were torn and shredded, feathers scattered around him like dying embers. The earth seemed to recoil around him, rain hissing as it struck his flesh.

A winged celestial.

A creature of the old prophecies.

His eyes flickered open—silver, dulled by pain. "Help me," he rasped.

Anya should have run. The warnings were carved into her bones, passed down in whispers from birth.

Beware the winged ones.

Should one fall, so shall we.

The prophecy had haunted the coven for generations, foretold by their vampiric seer centuries ago. No one had seen an angel in all that time. Many didn't even believe they existed. They were myth. Legend. Omen.

But Anya couldn't turn away.

She saved him.

And it was the worst mistake of her life.

Bringing him back had been a battle in itself. The coven erupted in chaos the moment his wings crossed the threshold of their hidden sanctuary.

"You brought *that* here?" her mother spat, fangs bared, voice trembling with fury and fear.

"He was dying," Anya said, soaked and breathless, blood smeared across her arms. "He's alone. He begged for help."

"You don't know what you've done," her father said, voice tight with barely restrained horror. "The seer's words... You've invited a curse into our home."

"He's not what the prophecy warned of," Anya insisted, though her voice faltered under the weight of a dozen glares. "He's broken. If he were truly divine, he wouldn't be crawling through the dirt."

The coven murmured, some retreating from the room altogether. Others watched the unconscious stranger with eyes full of dread, muttering old prayers under their breath.

"No wings are to be trusted," her mother said coldly. "Light or dark. Heaven or hell. Their war is not ours."

"But what if he's not here to *bring* war?" Anya argued. "What if he's running from it?"

Her mother stepped close, voice dropping. "We were taught to fear them for a reason. You've read the texts. The seer said we would not recognize our doom until it was too late—and that it would wear the face of salvation."

"Then I'll take responsibility," Anya said quietly.

Her father's eyes narrowed. "You would stake your life on the mercy of a creature who once stood beside gods?"

Anya nodded.

The silence that followed was heavy. Tense.

Then her mother spoke, bitter and sharp.

"Very well. He lives—for now. But he does not leave your sight, Anya. Not for a moment. If he turns on us, the blame will not fall on prophecy. It will fall on you."

Anya bowed her head. "Understood."

And as the fallen angel lay unconscious, his broken wings twitching in some fevered dream, the coven watched in silence —terrified, wary, and waiting for the first sign that the prophecy had begun.

At first, Lorien was nothing but a wounded creature, weak and silent. The healers tended to him, binding his wounds, using magic to mend his broken form. Anya stayed by his side, watching him fight through the pain.

One evening, when the coven halls had fallen into a rare hush, Anya found Lorien standing alone at the edge of the cliffs, where moonlight carved the forest below into shadows and silver. His wings—still tattered and healing—twitched slightly in the breeze. His back was to her, shoulders stiff with thought.

"You shouldn't be out here," she said, approaching cautiously. "You're still healing."

He didn't turn right away. "I needed air." His voice was quiet but firm. "I've never handled cages well."

Anya crossed her arms. "You're not caged. We saved your life."

He turned his head slightly, silver eyes gleaming in the dark. "Did you?" A pause. "Or did you delay the inevitable?"

She frowned. "That's ungrateful."

"I'm not ungrateful," he said, finally facing her. "I'm... surprised. You could've left me there. Most would have."

Anya shifted her weight, uneasy beneath his gaze. "You were bleeding out in the rain. I couldn't just walk away."

He studied her, expression unreadable. "Your coven thinks you're reckless. Naive. A traitor, maybe."

"They're wrong," she said quietly. "You were hurt. That's all I saw."

Lorien looked back toward the horizon, the wind stirring long strands of ashen-gray hair across his face. "I was hurt long before you found me, Anya. Long before the gods threw me out like ash."

"What did you do?" she asked.

His hands flexed at his sides. "I questioned them. I believed power should be used to protect the broken, not to preserve the hierarchy. I spoke of change. They called it rebellion."

Anya's brow furrowed. "Did you fight them?"

"I tried to reason first," he said. "But they don't listen to reason. They only listen to obedience." His voice turned sharp. "I believed we could build something better. Something fairer. I believed they'd see the good in it, eventually."

"But they didn't," she murmured.

"No," he said bitterly. "They cast me down. Called me dangerous." A beat passed. "Maybe I am."

Anya stepped beside him, arms loose at her sides. "That doesn't mean you were wrong."

He glanced at her, searching her face as if looking for a lie she hadn't told yet.

"Maybe," she added, "you just trusted the wrong gods."

That pulled a small, humorless breath from him—almost a laugh. "Or maybe I trusted too much in mercy."

They stood in silence, side by side. The wind whispered through the trees far below.

Then, softer: "I still believe I can fix it," Lorien said. "If I can shape something *better*—something worthy—they'll see. They'll have to see. And maybe then..." He trailed off, shaking his head. "Never mind."

Anya tilted her head. "You think the gods will take you back?"

His expression darkened slightly. "They should."

She didn't know how to answer that. So she said nothing.

For a moment, the guard he always wore slipped. And in the glint of his silver eyes, she saw not power—but pain. Not cruelty, but conviction.

But that's when Anya's world came crashing down.

The grand hall of the coven—once a sanctuary—was now a slaughterhouse. The scent of blood and burning torches filled the air, thick and suffocating.

Anya stood frozen, breath sharp and shallow.

Lorien stood at the center of it all—wings unfurled, eyes

glowing like the edge of a blade. Not with rage. Not with madness.

With conviction.

Her parents knelt before him, regal even in defeat. The ancient leaders of the vampire coven. Her mother met Lorien's gaze with defiance. Her father said nothing, but his stillness spoke volumes.

"This didn't have to happen," Anya whispered, voice shaking. "You said you wanted peace."

"I did," Lorien said, his voice steady. "But peace cannot exist where fear is law. Your coven clings to superstition—prophecy masquerading as truth. They saw my wings and decided I was a curse. They would have killed me the moment you looked away."

"You don't know that!" she snapped. "You *don't* know what they would have done!"

He looked at her then, and there was sorrow in his eyes.

"I know fear, Anya. I've lived in its shadow. I thought I could break the gods' chains and make a better world. I failed then because I trusted too much in mercy." His gaze fell to her parents. "I will not make that mistake again. I was cast out for defying them. The gods. I thought I could offer a better way— free will, justice, peace." His fists clenched. "They called it arrogance. They called me dangerous. And they were right."

He turned to Anya now. "But I didn't give up. I believed that if I could shape something new… something *better*, maybe they would see. Maybe they would understand I was never trying to destroy their order—only mend what they broke."

Her father spat on the ground. "You think murdering innocents will earn back their favor?"

"I think letting the rot continue would prove them right about me," Lorien said, voice trembling. "I had to make a choice. So did you."

He stepped closer. Dark light stirred at his fingertips—not malevolent, but resolute. Controlled.

"Your parents refused peace. Refused progress," he said, voice low, firm. "I offered them a future. A new order. But they chose tradition. They chose fear."

"You *chose* this," Anya snapped, trembling. "You chose power over mercy."

"I chose hope," Lorien replied, not backing down. "Hope that the gods would see I could do what they would not. That I could *fix* what they abandoned."

Tainted light coiled at his fingertips.

"No!" Anya lunged forward, but strong arms seized her from behind, dragging her back

Her mother turned to her—one final look. There was no fear in her eyes. Only love. And regret.

The tainted light struck.

A crack like the snapping of bone echoed through the hall.

Her mother fell.

Her father followed.

Lifeless. Gone.

A choked sob tore from Anya's throat. Her knees hit the floor. Her mind reeled. *No.*

Lorien turned to her older brother. "The coven must endure," he said coldly. "But not like this. Not under their corruption. Prove your loyalty. End the cycle. End the lies."

Her brother trembled, fists clenched, but his eyes were already wet. "I… I can't."

Lorien's expression darkened. "Then you will show them what disobedience costs."

A whip cracked. A scream split the air.

Anya screamed too, the sound raw, feral.

"You would have died without us!" she cried. "I *saved* you! And this is how you repay us?"

Lorien turned toward her then, and—for the briefest moment—there was sorrow in his eyes. A shadow of something lost.

"You gave me shelter," he said quietly. "And for that, I owe you honesty. Your kindness blinded you. You believed your world was unshakable. But it was already rotting from the inside."

He stepped forward. "I didn't destroy your coven. I revealed its truth. I pulled down the veil. I gave it the chance to become *more*."

Anya's breath hitched. "You murdered my family."

"I freed your people from stagnation," Lorien whispered. "You'll see that one day. I've done you a favor."

Tears blurred her vision, rage burning hot beneath the grief. "No wonder the gods cast you out."

His wings flinched—ash-gray and heavy—as if her words struck somewhere deeper than bone. "No," he said. "They were wrong. They *will* see what I've done here. They'll see I was right all along."

His voice cracked—just slightly—but his silver eyes gleamed with conviction.

"They will open their gates again. I will walk among them once more."

Anya took a step back. Then another. No one stopped her. The guards were still, unsure. Lorien's gaze shifted back to her brother.

Run, something in her whispered. *Run now.*

She turned, bolting for the side corridor—the catacombs.

"Stop her!" Lorien roared, but the words came distant and fractured, drowned by the pounding in her ears.

She ran. Down winding tunnels of dust and death. Past coffins, sigils, and ancestral bones. Her legs burned. Her chest cracked with grief. But she didn't stop.

Not until the forest swallowed her whole, and the coven was nothing but a nightmare carved in blood.

And as she fled into the dark, one terrible truth settled cold in her chest:

Lorien may not have looked like a monster.

But he had become one—

Not because he *wanted* to destroy.

But because he still believed he was saving them.

11

Anya's feet pounded the forest floor, each desperate step a silent plea for survival. Smoke clung to her clothes, thick and bitter, the last breath of a coven she'd left behind in ruin. Her gray eyes flashed crimson as she pushed herself harder, short black hair whipping across her face.

Guilt coiled tight around her ribs. She had left her brother. Left him to whatever fate Lorien had carved from shadow and fire. The thought gnawed at her. Hollowed her.

She should have stayed. Fought. Died with them.

But she hadn't.

"You keep running, Anya." Lorien's voice drifted through the trees behind her—not mocking, but cold, resolute. "But all you're running from is purpose."

She didn't answer. She couldn't.

The air behind her shifted—cooling, tightening. She could feel him gaining, every beat of his massive wings slicing through the night.

"You and I could have built something eternal," he called again. "Something worthy of the gods themselves."

Anya snarled. "You slaughtered my parents!"

His response came swiftly, without hesitation. "A necessary sacrifice for a vision greater than either of us."

The thunderous beat of wings grew louder. Her heart slammed against her ribs. She pushed harder, thorns slashing at her legs, branches tearing her skin. Moonlight vanished as a great shadow swept overhead.

Lorien landed in front of her.

His ashen wings spread wide, cutting off her path. His eyes glowed. He looked like judgment itself.

"Did you truly think you could outrun an angel?"

She stumbled to a halt, too late to pivot. Her foot caught a root, and she crashed to the ground, the forest floor tearing at her skin. Before she could scramble up, he was above her—imposing and still.

"It doesn't have to be this way," he said. "You've seen the cracks. The fear. The lies they told to keep power in the hands of the old and weak. We could reshape the world, Anya. Together."

She looked up at him, eyes burning. For a heartbeat, she hesitated.

Then came the memories. Her father's face as the light struck him. Her mother's final breath.

"Never," she spat. "I'd rather burn than become like you."

Lorien's expression faltered—only for a moment—but then he straightened. "You still don't understand. I was cast down for daring to see the flaws in their design. I rebelled so others wouldn't have to suffer in silence. I thought… if I could build something better, the gods might see I was right."

Anya pushed herself up, standing eye to eye with him now. "All you've built is a graveyard."

"You think I wanted blood?" he said, voice rising. "I wanted *change*. Your coven ruled through fear. They bowed to prophecy. I offered them something greater—and they spat in my face."

"You offered obedience," she hissed. "To *you.* Not to anything righteous."

He stared at her for a long moment.

"And yet, you're still alive," he murmured. "Because I *spared* you. Because somewhere, I thought you might understand."

"I don't need your mercy," she growled.

With a burst of speed, she vanished into the trees.

Behind her, Lorien's roar shook the branches.

She didn't stop.

She ran until her breath burned and her legs threatened to give. She ran until the river rose before her. Without thinking, she dove in. The cold slammed into her bones. She let the current pull her downstream, let it strip her scent from the air.

When she clawed her way out on the opposite bank, the forest around her was eerily quiet. Drenched and shivering, she staggered through the trees until she saw it:

A village. Human. Flickering with torchlight and the warm glow of hearths.

Fear tightened her chest. Her coven had warned her—never step foot in human towns. If they discovered what she was…

She stayed in the shadows, silent as mist.

She didn't need their food. She didn't need their help.

But gods, she needed to stop running.

She crept through the outskirts, watching the slow shuffle of lives so different from her own. The ache inside her had nothing to do with hunger.

It was loss—thick and constant.

I can't keep running, she thought. *But I can't go back. There's nowhere left to go.*

The screams echoed in her skull. The fire. The moment her brother's hand slipped from hers.

"I should have fought harder," she whispered.

But even as guilt clawed at her throat, something sharper rose within—rage. Grief. And the quiet ember of survival that refused to die.

She clenched her fists.

"No," she breathed. "I won't let it end here."

She slipped deeper into the village, her movements silent, her senses sharp. Every flicker of torchlight and whisper of human life kept her pressed to the shadows. Her kind didn't belong here. If they discovered what she was, they wouldn't hesitate to drive a stake through her heart.

But Lorien wouldn't follow her into a human village. Not yet. Not when he believed she was still running.

That was why she had to stay.

She found a crumbling house at the edge of town—long abandoned, its shutters broken, its door hanging loose on rusted hinges. It wasn't much, but it was shelter. It was hidden.

And more importantly, it was *unexpected.*

Inside, she found nothing but dust, rot, and the cold scent of mold. Still, she wedged a broken chair against the door and collapsed against the wall, her limbs aching, her mind frayed.

"Lorien," she muttered, the name scraping her throat like ash. "Why couldn't you just leave us be?"

A creak of wood. She tensed. Listened.

But it was only the wind.

She let her head fall back, letting the shadows swallow her.

Just a moment, she promised herself. Just a moment of rest.

Her last thought before sleep claimed her was of silver eyes and burning wings, chasing her through a world she no longer recognized.

She would never truly be free.

12

Emmaline strolled through the bustling marketplace, the scent of fresh bread and ripe fruit heavy in the air. She paused at a vendor's stall, fingers brushing a bright red apple—just enough of a snack before heading to the guild hall.

A sharp noise cut through the morning chatter—a scuffle in the alley behind the butcher's stall.

Then came the sound of someone whimpering.

Emmaline's instincts flared. She stepped away from the crowd and followed the noise, weaving between crates and hanging cloths. As she rounded the corner, she caught sight of a young man pressed against the wall, clutching his neck, eyes wide with fear.

Standing over him was a figure cloaked in shadows. A girl—young, sharp-eyed, wild. Her posture was tense, defensive, but something about her made the hairs rise on the back of Emmaline's neck.

The girl's mouth was stained with red.

"Hey!" Emmaline shouted.

The girl turned. Blood smeared the corner of her lip.

And Emmaline understood.

The girl bolted.

"Stop!" Emmaline surged forward, her boots striking stone. She darted through the winding back alleys, chasing the stranger as she vaulted over barrels and ducked under hanging laundry. The crowd hadn't noticed anything. Not yet.

But *she* had.

The girl was fast. Too fast.

Emmaline pushed harder. She was a Slayer—trained to face far worse. She had faced miscreants twisted by dark magic. But something about this girl felt different.

The chase ended in a quiet courtyard.

The girl stumbled to a stop, chest heaving. She turned just as Emmaline skidded to a halt a few feet away.

"Don't come closer," the girl warned, voice low and sharp.

Emmaline held up her hands. "I'm not here to hurt you."

Her gaze swept over the stranger—pale skin, crimson-ringed eyes, blood still wet on her chin. She wasn't twisted. Not corrupted. Not lost.

She was hiding.

The girl backed against a wall, fangs faintly visible, breath ragged. Her posture was all tension, coiled to strike or flee. Emmaline stood across from her, unmoving—arms slightly raised, not in threat, but in warning.

"You're playing hero in a world that doesn't deserve saving," the girl snapped.

"Maybe," Emmaline said evenly. "But I won't stand by while someone throws themselves to the wolves. If you want to prove you're different from the ones who took from you, you don't become like them."

The girl laughed—cold and bitter. "Different? I drank his blood. You saw what I am. How do you know I haven't already become one of them?"

"Because you stopped."

Her breath quickened. "You don't know what I've been through. You don't know what I've done."

"Then tell me," Emmaline said softly—calm, but not pitying.

The girl narrowed her eyes, searching Emmaline's face like she was waiting for it—disgust, fear, the flinch. But it didn't come. Just silence.

Finally, she muttered, "I didn't choose this. Everything I loved was taken from me. And it was my fault."

Emmaline didn't approach, but her voice softened. "That doesn't have to define you."

The girl scoffed, eyes flashing. "And what do you think I'm supposed to do now? Join your noble cause? Pretend I'm something I'm not?" Her gaze flicked to the emblem stitched onto Emmaline's cloak. "You're a Miscreant Slayer. You're trained to kill things like me."

"If I thought you were beyond saving," Emmaline replied, "you'd already be dead."

That landed. The girl flinched—just slightly. "So what is this? Mercy?"

"No. This is me seeing something in you you've forgotten how to see in yourself."

She backed away. "I don't trust you."

"Then don't," Emmaline said. "But I'm not walking away. Not while you're still here."

"Why?" the girl demanded. "Why help me? You don't even know who I am."

"Because I know what it's like to feel lost." Emmaline's voice tightened, close to truth. "To feel like the world made a mistake keeping you alive. That no one sees you. That maybe you aren't worth saving." She paused. "But you are."

Silence bloomed between them, stretching long and taut.

The girl turned away slightly, her fists trembling. "You have no idea what I've done. The things I've let happen. Everyone who's tried to help me—" Her voice cracked. "They're all dead."

Emmaline stepped forward, careful. "Then let's not save each other," she said. "Let's fight together instead."

The girl shook her head. "I don't know how. I don't even know who I am anymore."

"That's okay." Emmaline extended her hand. "You just have to try."

The girl stared at it like it was a trap. Her jaw tightened. Her eyes shimmered with something caught between warning and want.

Then, slowly—warily—she took it.

"I don't know if I can be who you think I am."

Emmaline nodded. "You don't have to be. Just survive long enough to find out."

Something shifted. Not forgiveness. Not trust.

But the first flicker of something that might grow into both.

And for the first time in weeks, the future didn't seem quite so empty.

"What's your name?" Emmaline asked gently.

The girl hesitated. "Anya."

"I'm Emmaline."

Only the soft hum of the market echoed in the distance.

"You can't stay here," Emmaline said. "If someone else had found you—"

"But *you* did," Anya cut in, her eyes studying Emmaline's face. "So what now? You drag me to your guild? Burn me in the square?"

"No." Emmaline's reply was quiet. Firm. "I'm offering you a choice."

Anya gave a tired, humorless laugh. "I don't trust your kindness."

"You don't have to. Just… don't run."

Anya's expression darkened. "Why are you doing this?"

Emmaline paused. "Because I've seen monsters. Real ones. And you're not one of them."

Anya looked away. "You don't know me."

"Then let me."

A long silence passed between them.

And for the first time in a long while, the future didn't seem quite so empty.

———

13

The guild hall buzzed with activity, the clinking of mugs and the hum of conversation filling the air. Months had passed since Anya had arrived in the village, and in that time, she and Emmaline had formed an unbreakable bond. At first, Anya had been wary—sharp-tongued, defensive—but Emmaline's relentless kindness and quiet strength had chipped away at her walls.

What began as reluctant cooperation had grown into something far deeper: friendship, loyalty, trust.

Anya moved through the throng of patrons with ease now, a tray of tankards balanced in one hand. Her sarcasm had become a guild-wide amusement, and though few knew her past, her presence had become part of the rhythm of daily life.

"Watch your step, love," she quipped, sidestepping a drunken guild member. "Wouldn't want you to lose what little balance you have left."

Across the hall, Emmaline watched with a quiet smile. It amazed her how easily Anya had adapted. The scars were still there—Emmaline could see them in the quiet moments, in the haunted glances—but Anya was healing. She had found purpose. Belonging.

And only Emmaline knew the truth.

No one else knew what Anya truly was. A vampire. A secret they had both agreed to keep.

But peace never lasts.

A sudden commotion outside shattered the warmth of the evening. Shouts of alarm rang through the air, followed by the shattering of glass.

Emmaline's head snapped up, her body already moving. She and Anya locked eyes across the hall, and without a word, they bolted for the door.

Outside, chaos reigned. A miscreant—a creature of warped flesh and dark hunger—towered over a cluster of terrified villagers. Its body pulsed with shadow, its claws slick with blood.

Emmaline didn't hesitate. Her metal staff crackled with sparks as she charged, striking with practiced precision. Sparks danced across the cobblestones as she deflected the creature's attacks, her movements swift and deadly.

Anya hovered at the edge of the fray, every muscle tense. Her instincts screamed to join the fight, to tear the beast apart—but she held back. She had kept her secret for so long. Revealing herself now could unravel everything.

But then the miscreant struck.

Emmaline cried out, a sharp gasp of pain as claws sliced into her arm, blood blooming against her sleeve.

Something in Anya snapped.

A snarl tore from her throat as she lunged into the fray. Her form blurred with speed. Fangs elongated. Her dark gray eyes burned like fire. Gasps erupted from the crowd as she landed between Emmaline and the miscreant, her nails lengthening into claws that tore through flesh and sinew.

The villagers recoiled in horror.

"A vampire!" someone screamed. "She's one of them!"

Heads turned. Shouts rose in panic.

Ralgar stepped into the chaos, his eyes locking on Anya. The head of the Miscreant Slayer Guild. Emmaline's father. His hand went straight to the hilt of his sword.

"Step away from my daughter," he growled. "Now."

Anya froze, breathing hard, blood staining her mouth. Her gaze flicked between the terrified villagers, Ralgar's blade, and Emmaline—who hadn't moved.

They know now, Anya thought. *They all know.*

The miscreant, weakened and feral, lunged one last time. Without hesitation, Anya spun and caught it mid-air. Her fangs sank deep into its throat. With a final, savage twist, the creature collapsed, dead at her feet.

Silence fell over the square.

Only Anya's ragged breathing remained. She turned slowly, trembling, and met Emmaline's eyes.

"I'm sorry," she whispered. "I never wanted it to come out like this."

Ralgar's sword lifted again. "You knew about this?" His voice was ice as he turned to Emmaline. "How long have you been hiding this from me?"

Emmaline didn't flinch. "Since the day I met her."

Ralgar's expression twisted. "You should have told me. You endangered everyone in this village!"

"She protected them tonight," Emmaline said. "You all saw it. She saved my life."

"She's a vampire," someone muttered from the crowd.

"She's *Anya*," Emmaline said firmly. "And she's more human than half the people here."

Ralgar's eyes narrowed. "She's dangerous."

"So am I," Emmaline snapped. "We all are. But I trust her."

He stepped forward, jaw clenched, and said low enough for only her to hear:

"This is exactly the kind of reckless, softhearted foolishness that got your mother killed."

The words hit like a blade to the gut.

Emmaline's breath caught. Her face paled—but she didn't move. Didn't waver. She swallowed hard and said louder this time, so everyone could hear:

"She saved all of us tonight. That should count for something."

Ralgar's grip tightened on his sword. Then, with a scowl of pure fury, he lowered the blade.

"This isn't over."

One by one, the villagers turned away, fear still clinging to their expressions. But none stepped forward to condemn her. The whispers were loud—but the doubt had been planted.

When the crowd dispersed, Emmaline turned to her friend.

"You should have told me," she said quietly, still shaken.

Anya swallowed hard. "I was afraid."

Emmaline hesitated, then reached out and took Anya's hand.

"I don't care what you are," she said softly. "And they shouldn't either. You're still you. And I still trust you."

Anya's chest ached. She had prepared herself to be hunted, hated.

But not this.

Not hope.

She squeezed Emmaline's hand.

"Thank you," she whispered.

And as the wind swept the blood from the cobblestones and the flames died down, something deeper settled between them —solid and unbreakable.

Trust.

EMMALINE & ZOL

14

The blue pendant glimmered in the flickering candlelight, cool against Emmaline's fingertips as she stood before her father's imposing oak desk. Its familiar weight offered a fleeting comfort amid the suffocating expectations pressing in around her.

"You understand the importance of this union, don't you, Emmaline?" Ralgar's gruff voice cut through her reverie, his gaze as unyielding as the steel of his blade. "Your marriage to Rowan will secure the future of our guild—of our very way of life on this forsaken isle."

Emmaline nodded, her golden curls bouncing softly. "Yes, Father," she murmured, though her mind wandered beyond the confines of the isle's shores.

Ralgar studied her in silence, his scarred face momentarily softened by something almost like concern. "I know this is not the future you would have chosen," he admitted, his tone gruff but not unkind. "But we all have our roles to play in keeping the darkness at bay."

"Of course," she whispered, the words leaving a bitter taste on her tongue. "I should prepare for the day ahead."

Ralgar nodded, already turning back to his endless reports. "Remember, Emmaline—duty before all else."

Emmaline's footsteps echoed on the cobblestones as she walked alongside her father through the village, the air thick with the scent of brine and decay. The villagers whispered as they passed.

"The Guild Master's daughter..."

"Betrothed to young Rowan..."

"A fine match... a necessary one..."

Each hushed word pressed into her skin like a brand. Her fingers found the pendant again, its familiar chill grounding her as she struggled to maintain a composed facade.

"You see, Emmaline?" Ralgar's voice carried over the murmurs. "The people look to us for stability. Your marriage will bring them hope."

Emmaline nodded silently.

Her gaze drifted to the remnants of the old square, where moss crept over crumbling stone. Once, she had stood there with her mother, her laughter ringing through the air. Now, only silence remained.

A sharp voice cut through her memories. "What's on your mind?"

Emmaline hesitated. "I was thinking about taking on more responsibilities within the guild. Maybe... assisting with more miscreant hunts?"

Ralgar's brow furrowed. "Absolutely not. It's far too dangerous. And with your betrothal—"

"But wouldn't it bring honor to our family if I contributed more directly to the isle's safety?" She forced steel into her voice, though her pulse pounded in her throat.

A heavy silence stretched between them. Then, at last, a weary sigh. "We will discuss this later. For now, focus on your duties as my daughter. And as Rowan's future wife."

Emmaline inclined her head, but her thoughts were already racing ahead. There would be no later. She had no more time to waste. She was determined to leave this island before that could happen.

As they continued through the village, Ralgar's pace slowed. Emmaline glanced at him, surprised by the momentary hesitation in his step.

"You remind me of your mother," he said suddenly, his voice lower now, almost wistful. "She was stubborn, too. Never could accept the way things were."

Emmaline's breath caught. It was rare for her father to speak of her mother at all. "And yet, she still married you."

Ralgar gave a short, humorless chuckle. "Aye, she did. And in time, she found purpose in her place. She grew to love this village, this duty."

Emmaline's grip on the pendant tightened. "But she wanted more, didn't she? Before..."

Ralgar's expression hardened, though there was something tired in his eyes. "Before she was taken from us? Yes, perhaps. But wanting something doesn't mean you can have it. This island demands loyalty. We survive because we follow the path set for us."

Emmaline shook her head. "That's not survival, Father. That's a cage."

He exhaled heavily, running a calloused hand over his face. "I only want to keep you safe, Emmaline. This world beyond the isle—whatever fantasies you dream of—it's not kind. The guild, this marriage... they protect you."

"Or they imprison me," she countered.

Ralgar turned to her, his eyes suddenly sharp. "You think I don't see it? The way you stare out at the sea like it holds the answers? I was young once, too. And I lost everything because I believed in something beyond these shores. Your mother, this village... we rebuilt what was broken. I won't lose you to reckless dreams."

Emmaline swallowed, her emotions warring within her. "I am not her, Father. And I won't be you either."

Ralgar's gaze held hers for a long moment. Then, he simply shook his head. "One day, you'll understand."

She doubted it. But she didn't argue. Not now. She had already made her choice.

As they neared the guild hall, her father sighed again. "Emmaline... just promise me you won't do anything foolish."

She hesitated, then forced a small smile. "Of course."

It wasn't a lie. But it wasn't the truth, either.

As he turned away, she pressed her hand against her mother's pendant, feeling the thrum of something deep in her bones.

One way or another, she would escape this place.

15

The Miscreant Slayer guild hall loomed before Emmaline and her father, its towering stone walls lit by flickering lanterns. Inside, the air buzzed with the clinking of tankards, bursts of laughter, and the murmur of battle-weary voices. It resembled a lively tavern more than a war room.

"I have matters to attend to," Ralgar announced gruffly. "Stay within sight of the guild hall, Emmaline."

He strode away without another word, leaving her alone in the shifting glow of the firelight. As his footsteps faded, Emmaline felt herself drawn to the quest board. The parchments called to her like whispers on the wind—promises of danger, coin, and, most importantly, escape.

A shadow fell over her. "Well, well. If it isn't my lovely bride-to-be."

Emmaline tensed. Rowan.

He reeked of ale, his once-sharp eyes clouded with drink. His carefully braided hair was loose in places, giving him a disheveled, dangerous look. He swayed slightly as he stepped closer, his presence suffocating.

"Rowan," she said cautiously, taking a step back.

He chuckled, a dark, humorless sound. "What? No warm welcome? No embrace for your future husband?"

His breath, thick with alcohol, burned against her skin as he leaned in too close.

"You look nervous, Emmaline." His voice was a low drawl, laced with possession. "Are you afraid of me?"

She forced herself to hold her ground, even as her pulse pounded. "You're drunk, Rowan. Go home."

He scoffed, swaying. "Drunk? Of course, I'm drunk. What else is a man supposed to do when his own fiancée spends more time chasing miscreants than planning a wedding?"

Emmaline swallowed her rising fury. "I am not a possession, Rowan. I have my own mind. My own choices."

His expression darkened, his grip tightening on the edge of the quest board. "Oh, do you now? And what choices would those be? Avoiding me? Ignoring your duty?"

She clenched her jaw, keeping her voice steady. "I am not abandoning anything. I am finding my own way."

Rowan's face twisted with anger. "Your way leads to ruin, Emmaline. And I won't let you throw away everything your father has built. Everything we can have together."

She took another step back, her fingers brushing against a parchment pinned to the board.

"You don't get to decide my future, Rowan."

His jaw twitched as he pressed her against the quest board. For a moment, she thought he might grab her, force her to listen. But then, with a bitter laugh, he staggered backward.

"You'll see," he muttered, shaking his head.

Without another word, he stumbled back into the tavern, leaving Emmaline standing there, her breath coming fast and shallow. She exhaled slowly, pressing a trembling hand to her pendant. Whatever Rowan thought, whatever her father demanded—she would not be caged. Not anymore.

A cool voice broke the tension. "Don't let him get to you."

Emmaline turned as Anya stepped beside her, her dark gray eyes gleaming with amusement. The vampire's presence was a welcome balm.

"Anya," Emmaline breathed. "I didn't hear you come near."

"One of the perks of being undead." Anya smirked. "Though it does make bartending tricky. Patrons tend to spill their drinks when I appear out of nowhere."

Despite herself, Emmaline laughed, the tension easing from her shoulders. She was grateful the villagers had finally accepted Anya as a miscreant.

Anya's eyes gleamed with excitement and caution as she passed Emmaline a parchment. "I think I've found something that might interest you," she murmured, voice tinged with danger.

Emmaline leaned in, her emerald eyes widening as she scanned the quest details. "An ice demon?" she whispered, a shiver running down her spine.

"Not just any ice demon." Anya's pale fingers traced the intricate sketches on the parchment. "It's responsible for the blizzard plaguing the village. And..." She hesitated, her usual sardonic tone fading. "There are whispers that it might be behind the disappearances."

Emmaline's heart raced. Fear. Exhilaration. A chance. The reward listed at the bottom of the parchment was staggering—enough to buy passage off the isle and then some. Freedom, tangible and terrifying, was within reach.

"It's dangerous, Em," Anya warned. "This isn't some run-of-the-mill miscreant. We're talking about a creature of legend."

Emmaline's fingers unconsciously traced her mother's pendant beneath her cloak. "Danger is nothing new to us, Anya," she said softly, memories of past hunts flashing through her mind. "And this... this could be our chance."

Anya met her gaze, understanding flickering in her gray depths. "Our chance to leave," she breathed, the words heavy with promise and peril.

"Together," Emmaline nodded, her resolve solidifying. "We made a pact, remember? To find a life beyond these cursed shores."

A rare, genuine smile curved Anya's lips. "As if I could forget. You're the only reason I haven't gone completely mad in this godforsaken place."

Emmaline reached out, clasping Anya's cool hand in hers. "Then it's settled. I take this quest, slay the demon, and we use the bounty to buy our freedom."

As their fingers intertwined, Emmaline felt a surge of strength. The oppressive weight of duty and expectation lifted —if only for a moment. With Anya by her side, even the most fearsome ice demon didn't seem so insurmountable.

"To new beginnings," Anya murmured, her voice carrying a flicker of long-buried hope.

"And the end of old nightmares," Emmaline finished, her gaze drifting to the mist-shrouded landscape beyond the guild hall windows. Whatever perils lay ahead, she knew this was the first step toward breaking free from the chains that had bound her for so long.

Anya's smirk returned. "Now go show that demon what you're made of."

As they parted, Emmaline felt Anya's presence lingering like a protective shadow. The quest, her dreams of freedom, the suffocating weight of her betrothal—all swirled together in a dizzying storm of hope and fear.

At the village's edge, she paused, breath forming misty tendrils in the frigid air.

A gust of wind whipped through her curls, carrying the faint scent of decay. Her emerald eyes snapped open, scanning the mist-shrouded forest.

"This is it," she said, her voice trembling slightly. "No turning back now."

She stepped forward, leaving behind the suffocating expectations of the village. The path ahead was treacherous, filled with dangers unseen. But as she ventured deeper into the forest, Emmaline felt exhilaration ignite in her chest.

16

—————

The howling wind whipped Emmaline's hair across her face as she trudged through knee-deep snow, each step a battle against the relentless blizzard. Her emerald eyes narrowed against the flurries, scanning the white expanse for any sign of her quarry. The ice demon had haunted her village long enough. The bounty on his head would bring her people safety—and her, freedom.

She gripped her metal staff tighter, the crackle of electricity along its length a small comfort. The cold gnawed at her bones, but she pressed on, breath fogging in the air, heart steady with purpose.

A flicker of movement.

Emmaline froze, pulse spiking. A towering figure emerged from behind a jagged outcrop of ice, cloaked in gleaming obsidian armor. He stepped forward, and the world seemed to narrow to the space between them.

She had expected a monster.

What she saw instead stole the breath from her lungs.

The demon's armor shimmered under the pale light, his

platinum hair flowing like threads of moonlight in the wind. But it was his eyes—piercing, glacial—that locked onto hers and sent a deeper chill through her than the storm ever could. For one suspended heartbeat, Emmaline forgot how to move.

This... this is the demon?

Her fingers tightened around her staff, uncertainty coiling through her. He was lethal. But something in her gut twisted, whispering that he was more than just a nightmare from the stories.

The demon studied her in silence. He had expected a hunter —another blade-wielding threat. Instead, he found *her*. The one his soul had been waiting for. The realization hit like a bolt of lightning. His mate.

But she didn't know.

Tension crackled between them like the storm overhead. Emmaline lifted her staff, its electric hum sharp in the hush. "I won't let you hurt anyone else," she said, breath curling in the frozen air.

He couldn't understand her words, but he felt the defiance in her stance. The fire in her eyes. It mesmerized him. Slowly, he slid his obsidian helmet into place, horns curving like a crown of warning.

Then he moved.

A blur of motion—daggers drawn, striking against her staff. The impact jolted her to her core. She steadied, sparks flaring as she countered.

He was strong. Terrifyingly so. Yet behind each attack, she sensed hesitation.

They danced in the snowstorm—ice and lightning colliding. Her electricity flared against his freezing might, the rhythm of their battle wild, unrelenting. His eyes never left hers. Not once. And though hers burned with determination, something unfamiliar and magnetic crept in.

Why is he holding back?

He could not bring himself to strike. Every instinct screamed *protect*, not *destroy*. But she didn't know—didn't feel it. She fought as though her life depended on ending his.

She lunged, staff swinging. He dodged, graceful and precise. Their blades clashed in a deadly harmony, a storm within the storm.

Then Emmaline faltered, chest heaving. Snow whipped between them. The demon stood just out of reach, studying her —not with malice, but with something… else.

She had come to kill a monster.

But she had met something else entirely.

And she wasn't ready to face what that meant.

His retreat caught her off guard. She blinked as he vanished into the flurry, and without thought, she gave chase. The wind cut her cheeks, her breath came in ragged gasps.

A crack.

The ice beneath her groaned, deep and ominous. Her boots struck hard—and then the lake shattered beneath her.

Frigid water swallowed her whole.

Pain shot through her chest as the cold gripped her lungs. Her weapons dragged her down, deeper into the dark. Her vision blurred. Her limbs slowed. The surface slipped farther and farther away.

Across the lake, the demon stood still.

He should turn away. Let the water take her. Let the bond dissolve before it anchored deeper.

But he didn't move.

Then, he *did*.

The storm obeyed him. The frozen lake surged upward, water bending to his command. Emmaline's body lifted, encased in icy shards, rising like a ghost from the depths.

She broke the surface, limp and deathly pale.

He stepped forward and caught her.

His arms wrapped around her, possessive, protective. He pressed trembling fingers to her throat.

A pulse.

Relief crashed through him.

He had saved her.

And bound himself to her.

The storm screamed around them, as if furious at his choice. But it was too late. The bond had begun to weave between them, invisible and inescapable.

He gathered her into his arms and turned toward the mountains.

She would live.

And he would face the truth he could no longer outrun:

She was his.

And he was hers.

17

The journey to the cavern was a blur of wind and white. Snow lashed against the armored figure's back, yet he barely felt the cold. Not with her in his arms.

The girl—fevered, fragile, warm—lay nestled against his chest, her breath shallow but steady. She should have been a burden, but he carried her as if she were made of something sacred. Breakable. Precious. The choice to save her had already stitched itself into the marrow of him, and still he could not explain why.

Not with words.

Not even to himself.

The mouth of the cavern loomed ahead, carved into the mountainside like a scar. The runes etched along its edge pulsed faintly as he approached, old magic stirred by his return. Accusing. Remembering.

You survived when we did not.

His jaw tightened.

He had made his choice.

With a wave of his hand, the ice barrier shattered—a burst of glasslike shards dissolving into the storm. He stepped inside. The wind ceased. Silence fell.

The cavern greeted him like a memory—frozen, glowing. Ice sheathed the walls, casting a pale blue light that danced across the jagged floor. Ancient stalagmites jutted like teeth from the ground, and the chill of a thousand ghosts lingered in the air.

He laid her gently on a wide, flat stone. Her cheeks were flushed with fever, her brow slick with cold sweat. A few strands of damp hair clung to her lips. He brushed them away with careful fingers, then turned to fetch a blanket—tattered, rough, stolen long ago from a forgotten village. He wrapped it around her shoulders, shielding her from the cavern's breath.

Then he sat beside her.

Watching. Waiting.

Days passed.

She stirred restlessly, murmuring words he couldn't understand. Sometimes, her fingers reached for him in sleep. Sometimes, they touched. And when they did—when her skin brushed his—something stirred beneath his own. A pull. A heat. A need.

He didn't understand it.

Only that it was growing.

When she finally woke, her breath caught in her throat. Her eyes—vivid green, glazed with confusion—snapped open and locked on him.

She flinched.

Scrambled back.

Her body collided with the icy wall, her hand flying to her chest. She scanned the cavern wildly, heart pounding in her ears. Then her gaze returned to the horned figure watching her from the shadows.

He raised his hands slowly in surrender.

Then, with deliberate care, unfastened the twin daggers at

his belt and laid them on the ground between them. Their metallic clatter echoed through the chamber.

He didn't speak. He simply watched.

She gripped the blanket tighter.

"You don't want to hurt me," she said cautiously, eyes flicking over him—his obsidian armor veined with frost, his curved horns, his eyes like glacier flame. "Do you?"

He shook his head.

Her eyes narrowed slightly, unsure if she believed him. "You can't understand me, can you?"

He said nothing. Just lowered his hands.

She followed his gaze to the carvings etched into the wall behind her. Hesitantly, she rose—legs trembling beneath her—and stepped toward them, brushing her fingers over one of the symbols.

It pulsed faintly beneath her touch.

"I've seen these before," she whispered. "In old texts. Before the miscreants came."

Then her knees buckled.

He was there before she hit the floor.

Strong hands caught her. Lifted her. Held her. Her body collided with his, chest against chest, breath tangling with his in the cold air. Her heartbeat stuttered. So did his.

She looked up.

His eyes were unreadable. But they didn't look cruel. They looked… torn.

She didn't pull away.

Not immediately.

Then she did. Slowly. "Thanks," she murmured, her voice unsteady.

He let her go as if her touch burned him.

The tension between them clung like smoke.

She glanced toward the cavern's entrance, where the storm

had dulled to a soft whisper. "I should go," she muttered. "My father will be looking for me."

He didn't stop her.

But he didn't move, either.

She turned back, wrapped in her blanket, and took a tentative step closer. "I'm Emmaline," she said. Her voice was firmer now, but wary. "That's my name."

The horned figure paused.

Then, slowly, he placed a hand over his heart.

"Zol."

The name echoed between them, reverent and raw.

Her lips parted. "Zol." She tried it again, softer. "Zol."

It felt like the start of something.

And the end of something else.

From that moment forward, the cavern became a place suspended between silence and something deeper. Emmaline healed. He taught her pieces of his language—scratched in frost, murmured in broken syllables. She taught him hers. They communicated in glances, in half-smiles, in the accidental brush of fingertips.

But the bond…

The bond was louder than all of it.

When their hands touched, it wasn't just warmth she felt. It was pull. Crackling energy beneath her skin. Her breath would catch; her heart would stutter.

And his eyes would darken with something he didn't understand.

One night, they sat by the fire, legs almost touching. Neither spoke for a long while.

Then she said, "Do you feel it too?"

He turned, slowly.

"This… thing," she continued, not quite looking at him. "Like I'm being drawn to you. Like I've been… tethered."

He said nothing.

But his hand moved.

Found hers.

Their fingers brushed.

Then curled together.

The contact was simple. But it scorched her.

"I don't know what this is," she whispered.

His gaze dropped to her lips.

"Neither do I."

And in the hush of the ice-bound cavern, something ancient began to stir.

Something inevitable.

Something waiting to ignite.

And then came the truth.

The miscreants that plagued the isle weren't born of evil. Some had once been Zol's people. Ice demons, like him. He had fought to protect them. Fought the darkness when it swept over the land, corrupting the weak, turning his kin into monsters.

But it hadn't been enough.

One by one, he had watched them fall—his brothers, his sisters, his father. His mother. He had watched his home shatter, swallowed by a shadow that knew no mercy.

And when it was over, only he remained.

Emmaline stood beside him one evening as he traced the final carving on the wall—an image of a woman with fierce eyes and flowing platinum hair. His mother.

"I'm sorry," she whispered.

He didn't answer.

He didn't need to.

As the blizzard finally began to ease, Emmaline turned to him, the firelight flickering across her face. Her voice was quiet, almost uncertain.

"Come with me."

His gaze flickered. "To your village?"

She nodded. "They accepted my friend, Anya. Maybe, in time, they could accept you too."

He was silent for a long moment. Then, slowly, he nodded. "We go. Together."

And as they stepped beyond the cavern into the fading storm, something unspoken settled between them. A bond woven in ice and fire, in grief and longing.

The path ahead would be uncertain.

Dangerous.

But for the first time in decades, Zol did not walk alone.

18

The village loomed ahead, a cluster of snow-capped cottages braced against the bitter wind. Emmaline's boots crunched over the icy cobblestones as she led the ice demon through the silent streets, her grip tightening around the metal staff at her hip. The air was thick with tension, the kind that clung to the skin and settled in the bones.

Whispers slipped through cracked doors and shuttered windows.

"Miscreant."

"Demon."

Emmaline caught glimpses of pale, wary faces peering out from behind curtains. Beside her, Zol walked in silence, his obsidian armor glinting faintly under the gray light. She didn't need to look at him to feel the unease rolling off him. It mirrored her own.

They reached the square. A crowd had gathered, a wall of wary eyes and clenched jaws. Emmaline stopped at the center, turned, and faced them.

"Please," she began, her voice louder than she expected,

steadier than she felt. "I know what this looks like. I know you're scared. But I'm asking you to listen before you judge."

Murmurs rippled. Someone scoffed.

"He's not our enemy," she continued. "Zol has lost more than any of us. He's not here to hurt anyone. He's here because I brought him. Because I trust him."

"You *trust* him?" someone shouted. "He's a miscreant! You've seen what they do!"

Electricity sparked faintly along her staff as the anger rose in her chest. "Yes," she said firmly. "I've seen what the darkness can do. I've *fought* it. And I've also seen the pain it leaves behind. Zol has suffered because of it—just like we have."

The crowd stirred. Some eyes shifted to Zol, then quickly away.

"People of Blackthorn," she said, louder now. "I, Emmaline Devereaux, Miscreant Slayer, stand here and swear that Zol means us no harm."

Beside her, Zol stiffened. She felt his gaze shift toward her, but didn't look back.

A hard voice cut through the quiet.

"What the hell is going on here?"

Ralgar Devereaux. Her father.

He stepped through the crowd like a thundercloud, broad-shouldered and storm-eyed, his expression carved from stone.

"Emmaline," he growled, "are you out of your mind? You bring *that* into our village? You disappear without a word? You have any idea what you've risked?"

"I had to," she said, her voice taut. "You don't understand—"

"No," he snapped. "*You* don't understand. Your mother died because of one of *them*. Have you forgotten that? Have you forgotten who you are?"

The words hit deep. As if she could ever forget.

The memory crashed over her like a wave, pulling her under.

She was six again, crouched behind the shattered remnants of a wooden table, her tiny fingers clamped over her mouth to keep from screaming. Her mother stood in the center of their home, blade in hand, facing the towering beast that had torn through the door. Its black eyes gleamed with malice, its claws slick with blood—her father's blood. The stench of iron and burnt wood filled the air.

"Run, Emmaline!" her mother had shouted. But she couldn't. She was frozen, watching as the miscreant lunged. She remembered the sickening crunch of bone, the way her mother's scream was abruptly cut short. The splash of red against the wall. The way her vision blurred as she choked on a sob. Then— nothing but silence. And the cold, suffocating weight of grief that had followed her ever since.

Emmaline blinked back to the present, her grip on her staff tightening. "I haven't forgotten," she said, voice tight. "But I also remember what you taught me: to think for myself. To see the truth, even when it's hard. Zol isn't the monster we were taught to fear."

Her father's hand shot up, aiming to strike her.

But it never landed.

Zol moved like a shadow—silent, sudden. His armored hand caught Ralgar's wrist midair.

Gasps echoed. The square went still.

Ralgar stared at him, eyes burning, but Zol didn't flinch. Didn't squeeze. Just held.

Emmaline stepped between them. "Stop. Please."

Zol released her father and stepped back.

"He's not the enemy," she said again, to everyone now. "The storms? The miscreants? They're symptoms of something worse. A darkness we barely understand. Zol's people were destroyed by it. He's *not* one of them—he's what's left."

The villagers shifted, uncertain.

"And what about Anya?" Emmaline asked. "You let her in. She was feared too, once. And she proved herself. Zol deserves that same chance."

A pause.

Then a voice cut through the quiet.

"And what of loyalty, Emmaline?"

Rowan Ashford.

He stood at the edge of the crowd, his broad shoulders tense, his brown eyes locked onto her with fury. "What of duty? To your people? To your betrothed?"

Her pulse spiked. Fingers clenched tight around her staff, she forced her voice to stay level. "My loyalty is to what's right, Rowan. To understanding. Not blind hatred."

Rowan stepped closer, fists clenched. "You defend a demon, and you speak of compassion? Have you forgotten what they're capable of?"

Emmaline's eyes flicked to Zol—silent, unmoving. The weak sunlight glinted off his dark armor, a stark reminder of his otherness. But he wasn't a monster.

"I haven't forgotten," she said quietly. "But I've learned to look past fear. Maybe it's time you did the same."

She turned back to the villagers, her voice carrying over the hush. "I know you're afraid. The isle has been dark for so long, it's hard to believe anything else is possible. But what if I told you the creatures we fear might be the key to our survival? Our histories tell of a time when humans and miscreants lived side by side. We can do it again."

She let the words settle.

"Zol is not our enemy," she continued. "He's a victim of the same evil that haunts us all. But together, we can fight it. Human and miscreant alike."

A shift rippled through the crowd. Anya offered a small nod of approval.

The tension in the air began to ease, like ice starting to thaw. Slowly, hesitantly, villagers murmured amongst themselves, curiosity stirring where there had been only fear.

But when Emmaline met Rowan's gaze, his fury remained, cold and sharp as a blade.

This battle was far from over.

s the murmurs of the crowd faded to a hushed hum, Emmaline sensed a shift beside her. She turned, meeting Zol's piercing gaze. The icy blue of his eyes had softened—just barely—a flicker of warmth breaking through the frost.

Zol's imposing figure seemed less rigid, the sharp angles of his obsidian armor no longer quite so threatening. He exhaled slowly, mist curling from his lips in the frigid air, as if some invisible weight had been lifted from his shoulders.

"Thank you," he said, his deep, gravelly voice almost hesitant, as though unfamiliar with the words.

Emmaline's heart swelled. "You're welcome," she murmured, resisting the impulse to reach for his arm. Instead, she gave him a small, reassuring smile, hoping he understood what she couldn't put into words.

A throat cleared nearby, breaking the moment. Emmaline turned to see her father, Ralgar, standing before them. His weathered face was hard to read, his expression caught between conflict and reluctant acceptance. His eyes flickered from her to Zol.

"Emmaline," he began, his voice rough. "I… I may have judged too quickly."

His hand rested on the hilt of Frostrend, his legendary warhammer. The weapon pulsed faintly with energy, the icy aura shimmering in the fading light.

"This hammer," Ralgar continued, running a hand along its cold metal, "wasn't always a weapon of division. Once, it was a symbol of unity."

Emmaline's brow furrowed. "What are you saying?"

Ralgar turned to Zol, studying him with new eyes. "Frostrend was forged by your people. By the ice demons. Generations ago, before the rift that tore our world apart, humans and demons lived side by side. This was their gift to us. At least, that's what the old tomes read."

Zol's stoic mask faltered, shock flashing across his face. "That… cannot be," he said, his thick accent rough around the words.

Ralgar nodded grimly. "It was before the darkness loomed over the isle."

Emmaline's mind reeled. The runes, the stories, the truth about the miscreants—it was all coming together like pieces of a shattered mirror slowly realigning. They were standing on the edge of something ancient, something bigger than any of them understood.

Then, like a blade slicing through cloth:

"How touching."

The voice was poison.

Rowan approached like a storm in human form, chestnut braid whipping over his shoulder, fists clenched at his sides. His brown eyes burned with betrayal.

"A history lesson and a demon's welcome party," he snarled, voice dripping with venom. "Is this what we've become?"

Emmaline tensed. She'd expected resistance. But not like this. Not from *him*.

"You can't be serious about this," Rowan snapped, stalking forward. He didn't stop at the edge of the gathering. He walked right up to her. Right up to *them*. "Have you all lost your minds? Or just your survival instincts?"

Uneasy murmurs stirred among the villagers. She could feel it—the fragile trust she'd built beginning to fracture under the weight of Rowan's fury.

"Rowan," she said carefully, forcing her voice to stay calm, steady. "You don't understand—"

"Oh, I understand perfectly." His voice cracked like thunder. "You've chosen *him*. A miscreant. Over your people. Over your *own blood*. Over *me*."

Emmaline's emerald eyes sharpened like a blade pulled from its sheath. "This isn't about you."

Rowan's lips twisted into a sneer. "Isn't it?"

He turned to the crowd, gesturing wildly toward Zol. "We've all bled to keep this village safe. We buried friends. Family. And now she brings the *enemy* inside our gates like he's some wounded bird we should nurse back to life?"

He rounded on Zol, eyes seething. "What's next? Do we let the other beasts in too? Invite them to our tables? Let them *breed* among us?"

Zol didn't move. But the air around him grew colder, the snow hissing as it hit the ground near his feet. His expression remained unreadable—but Emmaline saw the flicker of pained anger in his eyes.

"Enough," she said, stepping between them.

Rowan's gaze snapped to her. "You don't see it yet, but you've already chosen the wrong side."

"I see him," she said, her voice rising now. "I see *you*, Rowan. You say you want to protect the village, but all I see is your pride. Your fear."

"Fear is what keeps us alive!" he roared.

"No," she shot back. "Fear is what destroys us from within."

She turned to Zol, her voice softening. The firelight caught the glint of frost on his armor. "You've lost everything. But you still protected me. You could've let me drown. You could've left me to freeze. But you didn't."

His eyes searched hers, unsure, as if daring to believe.

And then she turned back to Rowan—deliberate, unyielding.

"I want him to stay," she said, loud enough for all to hear. "With me."

A beat of stunned silence.

Then chaos.

Voices rose in alarmed whispers, disbelief spreading like wildfire. But Rowan went still.

His jaw clenched. "You *what?*"

"I want him to stay in my home," Emmaline repeated, locking eyes with him. "Under my roof. As my guest."

It wasn't just an invitation. It was a declaration.

Rowan's face drained of color, then flushed with rage. He took a step forward—but Zol moved too, a subtle shift, silent and looming. Not aggressive. Not threatening.

Just *present.*

Rowan stopped.

"This isn't over," he growled, voice low and sharp enough to cut. "You may have forgotten who you are, Emmaline. But I haven't. And I won't let you burn this village to the ground just to prove a point." Rowan's eyes darkened. "You'll regret this."

Then he turned and stalked into the night, his fury trailing behind him like smoke from a dying fire.

The villagers were left murmuring, torn between fear and

awe. The air crackled with tension, thick and cold and uncertain.

Emmaline didn't waver. She turned to Zol.

He was still watching her—his gaze unreadable, but no longer distant.

"You would trust me so?" he asked quietly.

"I would," she said.

The crowd whispered, uncertain. She didn't care.

Zol stepped closer, his voice lower, rougher. "Even knowing what I've been?"

"I see what you *are*," she said. "And I won't let fear decide for me."

The moment hung between them, heavy with risk. With consequence.

But when Zol nodded once—just once—it felt like something old cracking open to let light in.

Emmaline knew what this meant. Not just for her. Not just for Zol.

But for *everyone*.

And when he stood beside her, silent and unflinching, she didn't feel afraid.

She felt *ready*.

20

As the weeks passed, Zol found it harder to stay in the village. Though Emmaline had opened the door to acceptance, the stares never stopped. The whispers followed him down every path, and even the warmth of firelight couldn't thaw the cold wariness in their eyes. But in his cavern—away from it all—he could breathe. There, he wasn't a monster. He was just... himself.

Still, Emmaline came to him often. Sometimes in the quiet of morning, sometimes long after the village had gone to sleep. Their moments together in the cavern were slower, quieter—filled with warmth that had nothing to do with firelight. They spoke in hushed tones, shared meals by flickering torchlight, laughed more than either of them expected. She brought bits of her world into his—books, bread, stories—and slowly, without either of them meaning to, their feelings deepened.

Whatever line had existed between them before was long gone now. What remained was something raw and real, a quiet devotion neither of them dared speak aloud—but both felt growing stronger with every shared breath.

Still, even with the comfort she found in those moments, Emmaline couldn't shake the weight pressing down on her chest, a storm of thoughts she didn't know how to weather alone.

She needed to talk to someone—someone who wouldn't judge, who could see past the fear and confusion. There was only one person she trusted with everything.

Anya.

She knocked softly on the door of her friend's cottage. It opened almost immediately.

"Em?" Anya blinked, already sensing something was off. "You look like your head's a hundred miles away. Come in."

Emmaline stepped inside, surrounded by the warm, herbal-sweet scent that always lingered in Anya's home. The place felt the same as it always had—safe. Like laughter and secrets were stitched into the very walls. It had been their hideaway, where they'd stayed up too late whispering about leaving the isle and seeing the world beyond the sea.

They settled at the little round table by the fire. A teapot steamed gently between them. Anya poured without saying a word, then pushed a cup toward Emmaline.

"Alright," Anya said gently. "Spill it."

Emmaline wrapped her fingers around the warm ceramic. Her hands were shaking.

"I'm pregnant," she said softly. "It's Zol's."

The silence that followed was sharp and immediate.

Anya froze. "Wait... are you serious?"

Emmaline nodded, biting her lip. "I've known for a while. I just... didn't know how to tell you."

Anya leaned back in her chair, blinking. "Wow. Okay. That's a bombshell." Her voice was calm, but the weight of the moment sat heavy between them.

Emmaline glanced down at her cup. "We made a pact,

remember? To get out of here together. To leave the isle. Start over somewhere else. I don't think I can go now. Not with the baby."

Anya was quiet for a long time. Then she reached across the table and squeezed Emmaline's hand.

"We were going to live in a tiny cottage on the coast," she said, a sad smile tugging at her lips. "Drink too much wine. Get sunburned."

"Name a goat after Rowan just to spite him," Emmaline added, laughing through the tears building in her eyes.

Anya chuckled. "A grumpy little goat with terrible hair."

They both laughed, but the ache didn't go away.

"I'm not mad," Anya said after a pause. "Not at all. I'm just... sad. This changes things. Not in a bad way, just... not how we planned."

Emmaline sniffed. "I feel like I'm letting you down."

Anya shook her head. "Never. Plans change. People grow. We'll figure it out. Maybe the dream looks different now, that's all."

"I don't want to lose you."

Anya's expression hardened with fierce emotion. She clasped Emmaline's hand tight. "You won't. If it weren't for you, I'd be dead, Emmaline. Dead, like the rest of my coven. You remember that day you confronted me? I was barely more than a shadow. I let the killer in—I trusted him. And it cost everyone their lives. I blamed myself. I wanted to disappear. But you— you didn't turn away. You stood there, in front of everyone, and gave me a second chance. You gave me a home. You made me believe I was still worth something. So don't you dare think you'd ever lose me."

Emmaline broke. The tears came fast, hot, spilling over before she could stop them. She leaned forward, shoulders trembling as Anya stood and wrapped her arms around her.

They stayed like that for a long moment—two souls clinging to what they still had, even as everything around them changed.

When Emmaline finally pulled away, wiping her cheeks, her voice was quieter. "No one's ever seen this before," she said. "A half-demon child? What if they don't accept the baby?"

Anya's smile faded. "We're going to need to be careful. Keep it quiet for as long as you can. No one needs to know but us and Zol. We'll make the rest accept this in time."

"That's the plan," Emmaline said. "But eventually, they're going to know. My cloak can only hide so much."

Anya hesitated. "What about Rowan?"

Emmaline looked away. "I don't know. It'll destroy whatever's left of our betrothal. Not that there was much to save. But when he finds out... I don't think he'll take it well."

"You think he'll get violent?"

"Maybe not at first," Emmaline said. "But he's proud. He feels like I humiliated him."

Anya exhaled slowly. "Then be ready. If things go sideways, you'll need to protect more than just yourself."

Emmaline nodded, her hand instinctively resting on her belly. "I know."

Outside, the village was quiet, but Emmaline felt the weight of eyes. The stares. The whispers that hadn't started yet—but would soon.

She pulled her cloak tighter around her growing belly, trying not to flinch when someone's gaze lingered too long. The judgment was coming. She could feel it in the air.

But she wasn't ashamed.

She just wasn't ready.

21

Months passed, and hiding became impossible. Emmaline's cloak no longer concealed the gentle curve of her belly. The whispers grew louder—louder than the winds that whipped through the village's narrow paths.

And Rowan began to notice.

He paced the village like a caged beast, restless, unhinged. His eyes tracked her every move. Each time she disappeared beyond the tree line, he followed with his gaze, fists clenching until his knuckles blanched. He knew something was wrong. Knew she was lying. And that knowledge festered like rot in his gut.

One evening, as the sun dipped below the horizon and shadows spilled across the ground, Emmaline hurried through the empty streets. Her heart thudded against her ribs, nerves pulled taut. The village was quiet, but it didn't feel safe—not tonight.

She reached her door, fingers fumbling with the latch.

"Emmaline."

She froze.

Rowan's voice—low and rough—cut through the silence like a blade.

She turned, and he stepped from the shadows, his expression hard, unreadable.

"We need to talk," he said, voice tight with restraint.

"There's nothing to say," she replied. "You need to leave."

He took a step closer. "You think you can just walk away from me? From us?"

"There is no us, Rowan. There never was."

His face twisted with something darker. Before she could react, he grabbed her wrist—tight, bruising.

"You don't get to decide that," he hissed. "You turned your back on everything we were. Everything I sacrificed."

She shoved at him. "Let me go!"

But he didn't. Instead, his anger surged. He forced the door open behind her, driving her backward into the cottage, and slammed it shut.

"Rowan!" she cried. "What are you doing?!"

He didn't answer. Just stepped forward, backing her into the wall. His hand slammed beside her head, trapping her.

"You think you can run to him?" he spat. "Give yourself to that creature?"

"You're scaring me."

"Good," he sneered, his dark eyes glinting with a twisted satisfaction. "Maybe you need to be scared, Emmaline. Maybe then you'll remember who you belong to."

"I don't belong to anyone!" she cried, struggling against him as his hands gripped her arms, pinning her in place.

Rowan's lips curled into a bitter snarl. "You've always belonged to me." He leaned in closer, his mouth brushing her ear as he growled, "And you'll *always* be mine, no matter how much you try to deny it."

Her heart thundered in her chest, fear clawing at her

throat as his hands moved down her arms. She twisted violently, trying to free herself, but his strength overpowered her.

"Rowan, please," she gasped, desperation creeping into her voice. "This isn't you. This isn't who you are."

But her words fell on deaf ears. His hand slid down, brushing against her stomach—and then he froze.

The tension in the room shifted instantly as Rowan's gaze dropped to her belly. His eyes widened, and his hands fell away as if burned.

"You're..." His voice cracked, barely above a whisper. He staggered back a step, his face twisting with disbelief. "You're pregnant."

Emmaline instinctively covered her belly with both hands, pressing herself further against the wall. She didn't trust the storm brewing behind his eyes.

"Yes," she admitted, her voice trembling but firm. "I'm carrying Zol's child."

Rowan's shock melted into something far more dangerous—rage. His nostrils flared, his fists clenching so tightly his knuckles turned white.

"You betrayed me," he snarled, his voice trembling with fury. "You gave him what should have been *mine!*"

Emmaline's chin lifted, but her voice was steady. "It was never yours to have, Rowan. My heart, my body, my *choice*—they've always been mine."

Her words seemed to snap whatever restraint he had left. Rowan surged forward again, his face contorted with anger, but she raised her hands to stop him.

"Don't!" she warned, her voice sharp and commanding. "You will not harm me, and you will not harm this child."

For a moment, it seemed like he might ignore her. His chest heaved, his eyes blazing with fury and something else—grief, loss, despair. But then he stepped back, shaking his head as if to clear it.

"You've ruined everything," he whispered, his voice raw. "You've ruined *me*."

Emmaline held her ground, even as her knees threatened to buckle. "Leave, Rowan," she said firmly. "Whatever you think we had, it's over. It's been over."

He stared at her for a long moment, his face a mask of anger and pain. Then, without another word, he turned and stormed out of the cottage, slamming the door so hard it rattled on its hinges.

Emmaline collapsed against the wall, her trembling hands cradling her belly as tears streamed down her face. The sound of Rowan's heavy footsteps faded into the distance, but the fear he had left behind lingered like a shadow in the room.

Outside, Rowan's mind churned. The betrayal cut deep, festering like an open wound. But deeper still was the voice—cold and insidious—that whispered promises of power, of vengeance.

And Rowan listened.

22

Emmaline's steps slowed as she approached the gathering of Miscreant Slayers. Their usual sharpness remained in their stances, their weapons never far from hand—but the eyes that turned toward her weren't hostile. Not anymore. Cautious, yes. Uncertain. But not cruel.

Whispers stirred between them, but the sting was gone. Something in the air had shifted. They saw her now—not just as the Slayer's daughter, not just the girl who had once blindly followed their code, but something more. Something different.

A voice, rough and familiar, cut through the murmurs.

"Emmaline."

Her heart skipped. She turned to find her father standing at the edge of the group, arms crossed over his chest, his expression as unreadable as ever. But his eyes—those storm-dark eyes—looked at her like they were seeing her for the first time.

"We heard about your... situation."

She hesitated, then let her hand drift to her belly. "I know it's not what anyone expected. But I'm not ashamed of it. And I won't apologize."

Ralgar didn't speak right away. He just stared at her, like he was sifting through every memory, every version of her he'd clung to, and letting them all go. Whatever he saw now... it wasn't the little girl he'd raised to hold a blade. It wasn't the Slayer he'd hoped she'd become.

It was *her*.

Finally, he exhaled, the sound rough in his throat. "I spent a long time trying to shape you into something I thought you needed to be. Thought it would keep you safe. Thought it would make you strong."

Her lips parted slightly, but no words came.

"I see now," he went on, softer, "you were strong the whole damn time. Just not in the way I expected."

Tears blurred her vision, sudden and hot.

"We've all made choices we believed in," he said. "Even when others didn't understand. I've made my share. Yours... yours just took more guts."

Her voice came out choked. "Thank you."

He stepped forward, slow but certain, and placed a calloused hand on her shoulder.

"I still think you're walking a hard road," he said. "People are going to whisper. Judge. Hell, some of them'll try to tear you down."

She nodded, swallowing the lump in her throat.

"But I won't be one of them. I've got your back. Always."

A single tear slipped down her cheek.

"And Em..." His voice dropped, just loud enough for her to hear. "If you believe in him... in this life you're building... then fight for it. But don't fight alone."

She nodded again, more firmly this time. "I do believe in him."

A long silence stretched between them, but it wasn't heavy. It felt full.

Ralgar's hand squeezed her shoulder once more before he let go.

"You've got a fire in you," he murmured as he turned to leave. "Don't let anyone snuff it out. Not even that hotheaded Rowan."

She laughed—a soft, tearful sound that broke through the pressure in her chest. Before she could respond, he was already disappearing into the crowd.

Her hand settled protectively over her stomach. The path ahead was still unknown, still full of shadows.

But her father had seen her.

And that was enough.

For now.

Rowan stalked through the village, each step striking the earth like a war drum. Frustration pulsed beneath his skin, building into something darker. Rage. Betrayal. The taste of loss was bitter in his mouth, and it festered like a wound left to rot.

The village that once felt like home now blurred past him in a haze of fury. He had given everything for her—time, loyalty, a future built on promises she had shattered. She had chosen him. He was sure of it. And then she'd thrown it all away for *that thing*.

His breath came fast, white in the frigid air. He stopped just shy of the tree line, the place he had seen her disappear too many times. Always slipping away. Always running to *him*. To the ice demon.

A tremor rippled through him as the truth he'd fought so

hard to ignore clawed to the surface. She was carrying Zol's child. That abomination. That mistake. That insult.

His fists clenched until the bones ached.

"I was patient," he muttered. "I waited. I *tried*."

But patience had its limits. And Rowan had reached his.

The wind shifted. Cold. Sharp. Unnatural.

A shadow stirred at the edges of his vision.

"Rowan Ashford," came the voice—rasping, ancient, laced with something unholy. It slid through the trees like smoke, like rot.

He turned, hand at his blade, but no blade could guard against this.

The darkness took form—something shifting, pulsing with malice.

"I felt it," the darkness hissed, drifting closer. "The fury. The grief. Delicious."

Rowan's grip on his sword tightened. "What do you want?"

But the shadow only laughed. "It's not what *I* want. It's what *you* want. You ache. You burn. You want her back. You want *him* gone. You want the child she carries erased from existence."

Rowan flinched, jaw tightening.

"You're nothing but whispers and shadow," he growled. "Why should I trust you?"

"Oh, you shouldn't," it purred. "But you *will*. Because you want answers. Because you want power. And I… I want your story. I want to know what she means to you. What *he* means to her. Tell me, Rowan. Let your hate guide you."

And he did.

He poured it out—every wound, every humiliation, every moment Emmaline slipped further from his grasp. He spoke of the child, the bond, the betrayal. And the darkness drank it in like wine, growing darker, deeper, heavier with every word.

"Good," it said. "So much pain. So much potential."

Rowan stepped closer, something inside him twisting. "You said you could help me. Make her forget. Make her mine again."

The shadows slithered closer. "Oh, Rowan. I can give you purpose. I can give you *power*. But not to change the past. Only to destroy the future."

"What does that mean?"

"It means she will never be yours," the shadow whispered, pressing against his skin like smoke and ice. "But you can make sure no one else gets her either. Not Zol. Not the child. Not anyone. All I need... is you."

Rowan hesitated—but only for a heartbeat.

"Take it," he said. "Take whatever you need."

The darkness surged forward, wrapping around him like a shroud. He gasped as something cold and ancient dug into his soul, threading through his mind like roots.

He screamed.

And then—he didn't.

The fear was gone.

The pain was gone.

All that remained was clarity. Cold, merciless clarity.

When the shadows withdrew, Rowan stood taller. Harder. Emptier. The man he had been was buried beneath something else now. Something worse.

The darkness receded into the trees.

"Go now, Rowan Ashford," it whispered. "Be my blade. My voice. My vengeance."

23

———————

The purple flames flickered violently, casting warped shadows across the walls of Conivx's chamber as she paced like a predator. Her alabaster skin drank in the unnatural glow, veins beneath pulsing with dark magic. Each step she took hummed with tension, fury coiled tight beneath her skin.

Behind her, chains rattled faintly.

Alikad stood at the edge of the chamber, shackled but defiant, the fire in his eyes dimmed yet unextinguished. He had escaped before, and each time, the chains returned stronger. But no chain could break the spirit in his bones—not yet.

The air shifted.

Candles snuffed out. A rotting cold swept through the room. The darkness had arrived.

"My lady," the disembodied voice rasped, its presence thick and suffocating. "I bring news I believe will... please you."

Conivx turned from Alikad, her irritation thinly veiled. "Speak."

The darkness's chuckle grated against the stone. "Zol, the ice demon, has bonded himself to a human. Emmaline Devereaux. She carries his child."

Conivx froze.

Pregnant.

The word clawed through her like a curse. "Between a miscreant and a human?" she snarled.

"Indeed. A blossoming love," the darkness purred. "A union of chaos. How poetic."

Conivx's mind twisted around the revelation. It wasn't just an alliance—it was a threat. A mirror of the betrayal that had torn her own soul apart.

"I should have ended that frozen wretch when I had the chance," she growled. "And now he dares to rewrite my history?"

The darkness curled around her like smoke. "This... entanglement may serve our purposes. Let them love. Love is fragile."

Conivx's gaze drifted to Alikad. Her voice dropped, bitter and low. "Kaeltharion. You chose my sister. You chose her over me."

Memories flared—Vespera's laughter, her glow, the child she bore in secret. The same child, now man, who now stood before her.

"You broke me once," she whispered to the memory. "I won't let it happen again."

She faced the darkness. "Tell me everything. Spare no detail."

"With pleasure," it hissed.

As the darkness spoke, Conivx approached Alikad. Her steps were slow, her expression softening into something darkly tender.

"Why do you continue to fight me?" she asked, her voice like velvet wrapped in iron. "We are alike, you and I. Power. Purpose. Blood."

Alikad's shoulders slackened with a suddenness that was

almost animalistic. He tilted his head, dark hair falling over one eye, gaze glinting with something too smooth, too rehearsed. But his voice… gods, his voice was silk soaked in poison.

"Perhaps you're right," he murmured, low and intimate. "Maybe I'm tired of resisting. Maybe I'm tired… of being alone."

Her breath caught. The truth of that hurt. He watched the way it moved through her, like wind curling around flame. She stepped closer, so close she could feel the heat rising from his skin. Her fingers, pale and ungloved, touched his jaw—just barely. A breath's pressure.

His cheek was warm. Too warm.

"Together," she said, voice no longer a command but a confession. "You and I could rule everything."

Alikad's breath hitched, lips parting slightly—eyes catching hers with a predator's glint hidden behind lover's longing. Her mouth was inches from his. His gaze dipped to her throat, lingering. Her pulse fluttered.

He leaned in. Their lips ghosted close.

And then—

A snarl tore from him.

The chains shattered with a scream of metal and magic. His arm blurred, a dagger conjured from nowhere, gleaming black as void, arcing straight for her heart. It wasn't just an attack—it was *intimate*. A kiss turned into a kill. The blade hummed with promise.

Conivx's eyes widened. For a moment—just a heartbeat—she didn't move. Didn't *want* to move. Not until the shadows screamed.

The darkness surged like a tsunami of ink, shadow-tendrils exploding outward, wrapping Alikad in twisting limbs. The blade froze, hovering a breath from her chest, just above her racing heart.

He roared like a beast denied meat. Her eyes shone—not with fear, but *fury*. And… betrayal.

"You ungrateful wretch!" the darkness bellowed, slamming him to the stone floor. His knees cracked against it, arms yanked back like a marionette caught mid-dance.

Conivx trembled, fingers curling into claws at her sides. Her lips peeled back, voice sharp and shaking. "After everything I gave you," she hissed.

Alikad snarled, teeth bared. "You gave me a *cage*. I just made you believe it was a throne."

His voice was venom, but there was something else behind it —something raw, aching. Real? Or just another lie?

The darkness loomed. "Enough. He must be sealed. In Limbo, his will shall fracture."

"No—wait." Conivx turned, her breath ragged. "We could… break him another way. Slowly. Keep him close." Her voice dropped to a whisper. "He almost fooled me. That kind of fire could burn for us, if… twisted the right way."

The darkness was quiet, pulsing like a heart made of tar. "No, Conivx. His defiance is not passion. It is rot. He must be cleansed."

Alikad thrashed harder, veins bulging, muscles straining.

Her lips parted. Something flickered in her. Guilt? Lust? Rage? It was impossible to name.

"So be it," she whispered at last, tears burning in her throat but never falling. "Seal him away."

The darkness did not wait. It *consumed*. Alikad screamed— not in pain, but *fury*. His cry was a curse, a promise. The shadows spiraled around him, swallowing his form until only the echo of his defiance remained, fading into the void.

Silence.

Conivx stood still, cold fingers brushing the air where his heat had lingered. She pressed two fingers to her lips—where his breath had almost touched hers. And then dropped her hand as though disgusted.

"What now?" she whispered hoarsely.

The darkness slithered beside her, forming a voice that dripped with icy logic. "He is gone. But not entirely. There is still a fragment—one we can mold. One who will obey."

She stared forward, eyes unfocused.

"Let me shape it." The darkness hissed.

She didn't answer for a long, long time.

"Do what you like. He meant everything. The rest is hollow."

She looked into the cracked mirror, saw the faint trace of the girl she once was. The girl who had loved. Who had been left behind.

She turned, spine straightening, expression cold.

Her mind returned to Zol. To Emmaline. To their child.

If love had broken her, then love would break them.

She moved to the ancient tome, its pages eager to obey.

"If love is their strength," she murmured, "then let it be their undoing."

Her voice rose in a chant:

"By shadow and blood, by pain and despair,

I curse this union, may they know no care.

When life begins, let life also end,

No mother, no child shall this birth transcend."

The shadows shrieked their approval as the spell sealed itself.

Conivx snapped the tome shut, her smile cold.

"Let love be their ruin."

$\mathcal{E}$mmaline's scream ripped through the candlelit hut, raw and full of agony. Outside, waves crashed against the shore, wind battering the wooden walls with unrelenting force. Inside, smoke from incense curled in the air, mingling with the scent of sweat and blood.

She was soaked in it—sweat, pain, fear. Blonde curls clung to her cheeks, her breath coming in ragged gasps as her body was wracked with another contraction.

"Stay with me," the village elder urged, her voice calm but eyes sharp with worry. "Your child's almost here."

"I can't—" Emmaline choked out, fingers clawing into the blanket beneath her. "Something's wrong."

The elder frowned. Then she saw them—dark marks, slithering across Emmaline's skin like ink in water.

"By the gods..." she whispered. "You've been cursed."

Emmaline's heart stuttered. "What? No—no, that's not possible."

"We must stop it," the elder said urgently. "Or you both won't survive."

Emmaline's hand flew to the crystal pendant at her neck—her mother's. It glowed, suddenly, fiercely. Light burst from it, searing through the gloom. The dark markings hissed and receded.

Zol burst through the door, breathless and wild-eyed.

"What happened?" His gaze locked on the marks fading from Emmaline's skin. "Who did this to you?" his voice was sharp, deadly.

"Dark magic," the elder said. "A curse meant to end both lives."

Zol knelt beside Emmaline, fury radiating off him in waves, but his touch was soft as he brushed hair from her sweat-soaked face. "I swear, Emma—whoever did this, they won't live to try again."

Emmaline reached for him, clinging to his hand. "I thought I was going to die," she whispered.

"You didn't," he said fiercely. "You fought."

And then, another scream. A final push. Her body buckled—but she gave everything.

The room fell still.

A single cry rang out.

"It's a boy," the elder whispered, voice shaking.

Emmaline collapsed back, sobbing. Zol supported her, holding her like she might slip away.

The pendant's light dimmed, settling into a faint warmth against her chest. Outside, the storm faded, the waves quieting as if the world, too, had been holding its breath.

She cradled her son to her chest, her voice low and fierce. "You're safe. I swear it. Nothing will ever hurt you."

The crystal vial exploded against the stone wall, shards scattering like tiny blades across the shadowed chamber floor. Conivx's scream shattered the silence like glass, raw and unhinged. Her violet eyes blazed with murderous fury, her entire body trembling with rage.

"Curse that insolent girl!" she howled, voice cracking under the weight of her hatred. "She should have died screaming!"

Emmaline's survival—her child's safe arrival—wasn't just an insult. It was blasphemy. A mockery of everything Conivx had endured. Her carefully crafted curse, forged in shadows and steeped in blood, had been reduced to nothing by a trinket. A pendant. A pathetic, glowing scrap of sentimentality.

The humiliation twisted inside her like a blade. It burned in her bones, throbbed in her skull. It consumed her.

She stormed across the chamber like a tempest, black robes lashing the air around her like snapping whips. Her hands curled into claws, nails digging into flesh until blood welled beneath her skin. She relished the pain. It was real. It was hers.

"I should've torn out that brat's heart myself," she hissed. "I should've strangled her with her own bloodline."

No more subtlety. No more waiting. She was done whispering through curses and pulling strings. This wasn't about strategy anymore.

It was personal.

With a violent slash of her arm, she summoned the darkness. Shadows ripped open a rift, twisting and coiling until the ominous presence formed fully before her.

"You summoned me," the darkness said smoothly, relishing her fury.

Conivx didn't wait. "Gather every miscreant. All of them. I want that cursed village burned to ash. Burn *every* village. Every human that breathes—kill them."

The shadows quivered with dark pleasure. "Every human?"

"Every last one!" she screamed. "This isle belongs to *me*! I bled for it. I *bled* for him!"

Her voice cracked, the old wound reopening. "Kaeltharion chose her. He chose my sister over me. And now *this girl* dares to live? To love? To build a life with a miscreant—just like they did?!"

Conivx spun toward the window, panting. Her reflection glared back at her in the glass—wild, unrecognizable.

"They betrayed me," she hissed. "He made vows to me and broke them. She pretended to care and stole him away. And now their legacy walks the earth while mine lies buried beneath it."

She pressed both hands against the cold stone, the world outside blurred by a storm of tears and hatred.

"Vespera's child should never have been born. He was supposed to be mine. My redemption. My revenge."

Conivx shook her head, fury trembling through her limbs. "No more second chances. No more stolen futures. Let the isle drown in ash and bone."

"End them all," she growled. "No survivors. Let them scream. Let their joy be ripped from their throats like mine once was."

The darkness bowed, its glee palpable. "As you command."

It melted into the walls, off to carry out her wrath.

Conivx stared down at the cursed earth, shadows writhing at her feet. Her power surged, fed by the raw fury of a soul betrayed by love, forgotten by gods, denied by fate.

She would not be defied.

She would be feared.

And by the time the fires died down, the humans wouldn't live to remember—this isle belonged to her.

And her hatred would rule it forever.

25

The darkness stood in the shadows, his form a shifting mass of shadow and malice, eyes glittering with cruel anticipation. Conivx's command echoed through his mind like a war drum. At last, the moment had come—total war on the isle.

With a smile as cold as death, the darkness whispered an ancient incantation, each word laced with venom. Dark energy pulsed outward, infecting the land like a sickness. His voice rose, summoning the miscreants from their lairs. Vampires, werewolves, demons—all awakened, their hunger sharpening with every breath. Even Zol felt the call, resisting with every ounce of will he possessed.

As the magic reached its peak, the darkness dissolved into the ranks of the rising horde. He would lead this chaos. Guide it. Amplify it. Tonight, the isle would burn.

But before fading into the shadows, he gave one final order —one meant for his most personal creation.

At the edge of the village, cloaked in shadow, stood Sirius. His white hair billowed in the wind, stark against the night. Pale as moonlight and cold as the steel he wielded, he looked like a specter made flesh—his yellow eyes glowing faintly beneath the shadows of his hood. His scythe glinted beneath the moonlight, a symbol of death incarnate. He had no memory of who he once was—only fragments of something broken. He had emerged from Limbo not as a man, but a creation, forged from a sliver of a soul too stubborn to die. The darkness had plucked that piece from Alikad's sealed spirit and given it new form.

Sirius.

He remembered only one thing clearly: the voice that found him in the void.

"Call me Father," it had said. And he had obeyed.

Trained as a reaper, Sirius followed orders. But tonight, as he watched the peaceful village bathed in silver light, something stirred. Not fear. Not hesitation. Something harder to define—guilt.

And then the voice returned.

"You will find her," the darkness whispered into his mind. "Emmaline Devereaux. The one who carries the child of ice. Hunt her. Spare no mercy. No quick death. She deserves to suffer—slowly, completely. A pain worthy of my betrayal."

He was told to kill. To erase. To destroy without question. But now, he was told to torment. To break her.

Miscreants emerged behind him—vampires snarling, were-wolves twitching with anticipation, demons trailing flame behind their steps. The storm was coming. He was meant to be its harbinger.

Sirius inhaled deeply and stepped forward.

The silence shattered. The horde descended. Creatures surged into the village, flames erupting, screams tearing through the night.

Sirius moved like death itself—efficient, silent, merciless. His scythe cut through those who stood in his path. But with every soul he took, the unease grew. The weight of their lives settled in his bones, foreign and heavy.

In the center of the chaos stood Ralgar, weathered and bloodied, defiant among the ruins. Smoke clung to his armor, but he did not yield. As Sirius stepped from the shadows, calm and cold, Ralgar raised his head.

"You've taken everything from me," Ralgar said, voice shaking with fury. "But you will not have her. Not my daughter."

Sirius tilted his head. "Your daughter? What is her name?"

Ralgar tightened his grip on Frostrend. "I'll never tell you. She's safe with that ice hellion."

"Ice hellion..." Sirius repeated quietly. Something in the phrase rang familiar.

Ralgar's heart pounded. Too late, he realized he'd said too much.

Sirius turned as if to leave, sparing him. But Ralgar made one last move. He lunged, raising Frostrend high.

Before the blow landed, a massive hand of shadow erupted from the ground, halting him mid-strike. The hammer slipped from his grip.

The darkness materialized beside Sirius.

"You fool," the darkness hissed in Sirius's mind. "He's her father."

Shock rippled through Sirius. Ralgar Devereaux—Emmaline's father.

"Zol is stronger than you know," the darkness warned. "Be wary, or even you will fall."

Sirius looked at Ralgar, studying him. The man's body was broken, but his eyes still burned.

"End it," Ralgar whispered. "Don't let her see me like this. Don't let her see what I've become."

The wind hushed. Fire crackled. The village was in ruins.

Sirius lifted his scythe, torn by the strange, unfamiliar ache rising in his chest. He didn't understand it. But he obeyed.

The blade fell.

Ralgar's body crumpled, his blood soaking into the earth. A father's final act of love.

And Sirius, forged from a broken soul, felt something shift.

For the first time, he wondered who he truly was.

And whether there was more to his story than death.

26

Emmaline burst into Zol's cavern, gasping for breath as if the air itself was burning. Her eyes were wide with terror, her face streaked with soot and tears. She stumbled, her blue pendant swinging wildly with each panicked step until she collapsed into Zol's waiting arms.

Zol caught her instinctively, his expression shifting from confusion to immediate alarm. Her sobs were muffled against his armor as he held her tightly.

"Emmaline," he breathed, brushing tangled hair from her face. "What happened?"

"The village…" Her voice cracked. "It's gone. Everything's burning. I—I saw a man dying in the woods. He told me to run."

Zol's jaw tightened, the light in his eyes dimming into something deadly. He cradled her close, whispering against her temple. "You're safe here. I swear it."

But inside, his thoughts spiraled. The flames. The attack. The darkness had moved. The guilt of his connection to it, however distant now, pressed on him like ice.

As Emmaline's breathing slowed, she lifted her head. Her

eyes shimmered with fear and determination. "We have to go back. There might still be survivors."

Zol hesitated. He wanted to say no. To beg her to stay. But he saw the fire in her eyes—and he couldn't ignore the truth. "Alright," he said. "But we go carefully."

She nodded, turning toward the small cradle tucked in the shadows. Their son lay there, wrapped in warmth and innocence. Emmaline reached out, her hand trembling.

"I'll come back for you," she whispered.

Then she turned, and they stepped into the night.

The sky glowed orange and red on the horizon, a beacon of devastation. Their footsteps quickened. Smoke thickened. Screams echoed.

The village was a battlefield.

Zol and Emmaline emerged from the trees, stumbling over rubble and scorched earth. Buildings crumbled. Flames devoured wood and stone. Miscreants flooded the streets like a swarm. The stench of blood filled the air.

And then she saw him—

"Father!"

Ralgar stood in the center of the chaos, hammer raised, frost swirling around him. Across from him, a tall, pale figure— Sirius. His ghostly white hair and glowing yellow eyes marked him like a phantom among the dead. His scythe flashed, wicked and beautiful in the firelight.

"NO!" Emmaline screamed.

She ran, lightning sparking across her metal rod. But before she could reach them—

Sirius moved.

With inhuman precision, he dodged Frostrend and drove his scythe deep into Ralgar's chest.

Time froze.

Ralgar crumpled. His eyes met Emmaline's across the flames

—apology, sorrow, love. Then he was gone.

She fell to her knees, choking on grief. Her screams tore the sky.

Zol reached her, his hand gripping her arm, eyes wild. "Emma, we have to go. Now!"

"I can't—" Her voice broke. "I can't leave him."

"We'll never make it if we stay."

She met his gaze. Saw her pain mirrored in him. Nodded.

They ran.

The village burned. And something inside her burned with it.

Zol turned, blades drawn. He tore into the miscreants with a fury that left ice in his wake. One by one, they fell.

Then the darkness emerged, laughter cold and echoing like splintered ice.

"You fight well, demon," he sneered, his voice curdled with glee. "But you cannot hope to defeat me. I am the one who brought your pathetic clan to its knees, the one who painted the snow with their blood."

The words ripped into Zol like jagged blades. Memories surged—his mother's lifeless eyes, his father's crumpled form, the village drenched in crimson and frost. Screams of the past mingled with the chaos of the present.

With a roar of fury and anguish, Zol lunged. His daggers gleamed with jagged frost, the air around him plummeting into a deadly chill. He slashed and parried, a tempest of vengeance and sorrow made flesh.

The miscreants swarmed him, claws and fangs snapping. Zol tore through them with relentless precision, freezing blood in their veins, shattering bones with a touch. Statues of ice and death littered the ground.

But for every monster he felled, more took their place. He was drowning in them.

"You'll die here," the darkness hissed. "And when you do, I will find her. I will break her slowly. Intimately. Until she begs for death."

Zol turned—Emmaline was gone.

Something inside him snapped.

A primal cry tore from his throat as a storm of frost exploded outward, freezing the battlefield in a ring of death. Miscreants shattered like glass. His power surged, wild and untamed.

He lunged at the darkness, blades drawn, fury incarnate. Their weapons clashed—ice against shadow, agony against ancient evil. The earth groaned beneath them, sparks flying from each impact.

Zol fought like a god undone, memory and reality bleeding together. He saw his kin's faces, heard their whispered pleas, felt their sacrifices urging him on.

He would not stop.

He could not stop.

Not until the darkness lay dead.

Not until Emmaline was safe.

Because she still lived.

And he still had something worth dying for.

27

*E*mmaline's heart pounded as she crashed through the smoke and ruin of the battlefield, searching for Zol. Screams tore through the air, fire consumed everything, and in the chaos—she lost him.

One moment, his hand had been in hers. The next, miscreants had separated them, driving a wedge of fire and death between them. She fought her way through the madness, calling his name until her voice gave out. Then she ran—blindly, instinctively—until she stumbled straight into *him*.

The monster who had just slain her father.

He stood amidst the carnage, ghostly white hair gleaming under the flickering firelight, yellow eyes unreadable, a scythe resting in his pale hands. A reaper made flesh.

Emmaline froze, her blood going cold.

"Why?" she demanded, her voice raw, grief and fury tangled in her throat. "Why did you do this?"

Sirius tilted his head. His voice was calm, detached. "It had to be done. Your people stood in our way."

"My father—" Her voice broke. "My people didn't deserve this."

"Deserve is meaningless," he replied softly. "We all do what we must."

Rage exploded within her. She lunged forward, her rod sparking with electricity. Sirius met her blow with eerie precision, his scythe clanging against the charged metal.

They fought. Sparks lit the air as metal clashed. Emmaline was relentless, driven by loss, but Sirius was faster—unnaturally so. He moved like death incarnate, emotionless and fluid.

"You're a monster!" she cried, striking wildly. "A heartless, soulless monster!"

Sirius's expression barely shifted. "Perhaps. But even monsters have their reasons."

"There's no reason for this!" she shouted, grief sharpening every swing.

Their battle raged, brutal and fast. She knew she couldn't hold out much longer. Then—

A hand grabbed her ankle, yanking her down.

Rowan.

His face contorted in a snarl, his eyes blazing with a malevolent light that sent a chill down her spine. She watched in horror as a dark force seemed to seep from his body, swirling around him like a noxious cloud. Smoke curled around him, a sinister aura radiating from his twisted form.

"Rowan?" Emmaline gasped, disbelief and revulsion mingling. "You... you were behind this. All of it."

Rowan's lips curled in a cruel smile, his grip on her ankle tightening until she winced in pain. "Foolish girl," he hissed, his voice dripping with contempt. "You never saw it coming, did you? Too blinded by your own naivete to see the truth that was right in front of you. You were supposed to be mine, Emmaline. MINE."

Emmaline's mind reeled, her thoughts scattering like leaves in a gale. How could she have been so blind, so trusting? She should have known he had been plotting against her, against everything she held dear.

The betrayal cut deeper than any physical wound, a searing pain that ravaged her soul.

But before she could even begin to process the enormity of Rowan's treachery, a flash of movement caught her eye. Sirius, his scythe a blur of silver, descending upon Rowan with ruthless efficiency.

There was a sickening crunch, a spray of crimson, and then Rowan was falling, his hand slipping from Emmaline's ankle as he crumpled to the ground. His throat gaped open, a macabre smile that leaked rivulets of blood onto the dusty earth.

Emmaline stared, transfixed by the gruesome sight, her mind struggling to reconcile the horror of what she had just witnessed.

He's dead, she thought numbly, the words echoing in the hollow cavern of her chest. *Rowan is dead. My father is dead. My people—are dead.*

Emmaline's heart hammered in her chest as she met Sirius's cold, unfeeling gaze. Fear gripped her tightly, choking the breath from her lungs. She took an unsteady step backward, trembling as the reality of her situation sank in.

The scythe in Sirius's hand glinted ominously, a cruel promise of death. "You can't escape me," he said softly, advancing slowly. "Surrender, and I'll make it quick."

She fled, ducking into a half-burned cottage. Her breaths came in shallow gasps. Her body screamed in pain, her vision blurred.

He followed.

Sirius stepped into the doorway, his cloak billowing like a shadow.

"Why?" Emmaline cried. "Why all this suffering?"

"I have no choice," Sirius said. "I am bound to obey."

"There's always a choice!" she screamed.

A flicker of something passed through him—regret? Memory?

"Not for me," he murmured, lifting his scythe, his yellow eyes glinting with grim resolve.

Emmaline's vision swam. "Mother, give me strength," she whispered hoarsely, summoning the last of her will.

With a defiant scream, she lunged.

The scythe met her with brutal grace, slicing through her side. White-hot pain erupted as the blade drove her to the ground. Her metal rod clattered uselessly to the scorched floor.

The impact knocked the breath from her lungs. Her limbs trembled, barely responding. Her eyes fluttered. She felt herself slipping.

Sirius knelt beside her, his pale face unreadable. He reached for the blue pendant at her throat.

Emmaline tried to lift her hand—failed. Her fingers twitched helplessly.

Then, the moment his hand brushed the pendant, something shifted.

His eyes widened. His hand froze.

Recognition.

A flicker of sorrow.

His breath caught, and for the first time, Sirius looked truly lost.

Slowly, gently, he lifted the pendant from her neck and tucked it beneath his cloak as if it were something sacred.

"I'm sorry," he whispered, his voice cracking. "In another life... maybe..."

He lingered a heartbeat longer, then turned away.

Emmaline lay broken in the rubble, blood soaking into the

scorched floorboards beneath her. The smoke, the screams, the horror—it all pulsed in and out like a dream she couldn't wake from. Her body was numb, her breaths shallow, but somewhere in her chest, her heart still beat.

"Zol..." she murmured, voice barely a whisper. "Our son... keep him safe."

Her eyes welled with tears as she stared at the broken beams above, flickering shadows dancing across the ceiling. "I'm so sorry," she breathed. "Please... forgive me."

The world around her narrowed. Her fingers twitched, reaching weakly toward the pendant that was no longer there. She blinked slowly, once... twice... then her eyes slipped shut for a moment too long.

But her chest rose again.

The fire inside her hadn't gone out.

Not yet.

nya's breath hitched. Pain surged through her body, every inhale a battle. Smoke curled around her face, stinging her eyes and filling her lungs with the stench of ruin. Screams echoed in the distance, a chaotic lullaby of fire and death.

She stirred beneath a pile of scorched rubble, pinned and bloodied. Her gray eyes fluttered open, blinking through the haze. Above her, the once-familiar ceiling of her cottage had collapsed, charred beams framing a sky blackened with ash.

Memories came rushing back—the attack, the screams, the way the sky had turned to flame. The horror of her home falling to darkness.

With trembling hands, she clawed at the debris. Splinters sliced her palms, but she pushed on. Her strength was fading, but her will refused to bend. Bit by bit, she shoved the wreckage aside and dragged herself upright, swaying on her feet.

What remained of the village stretched out before her in a smoldering wasteland. The air buzzed with heat and death. She staggered forward, heart hammering as she passed the fallen.

Old Mira, lifeless beneath the splintered remains of her porch.

Tomas, his blacksmith's hammer still gripped in a deathless hand.

Little Lily, her favorite doll melted beside her.

Anya fell to her knees, tears streaking down her soot-covered cheeks. "No," she whispered. "Please, no."

Each face carved a deeper wound into her soul. She couldn't stop the grief—didn't try to. It poured from her in waves, each sob heavier than the last.

"I should've been here," she cried. "I should've saved them."

A sound—a clash of steel against steel—ripped through the silence.

Her head jerked up.

Through the flames, she saw them: Zol, gleaming in obsidian and frost, locked in brutal combat with a monster made from darkness. Shadows and ice collided with earth-shattering fury, each blow threatening to rip the isle apart.

"By the gods," she breathed. Awe mingled with terror.

But then a thought punched through the haze.

If Zol was there…

Where was Emmaline?

Terror gripped her anew. She turned, scanning the devastation.

"Em!" she shouted, her voice hoarse. "EMMALINE!"

She ran—limping, stumbling, barely upright. Her scorched skin burned with every step, but she didn't care.

"Hold on, Em. Please."

A glint of metal caught her eye.

Emmaline's rod, twisted and bloodied, half-buried in ash.

Anya's stomach dropped. She staggered to it, kneeling as she lifted it with shaking hands.

"No…"

Her gaze rose to a nearby cottage—its door barely attached, hanging like a broken limb. She rushed forward and pushed it open.

The smell hit her first. Blood. Smoke. Death.

Then she saw her.

Emmaline lay motionless among the rubble. Her golden hair was matted with blood and soot. Her chest rose and fell in shallow, uneven breaths.

"Em!" Anya dropped beside her, hands cradling her head. "I'm here. I've got you."

Emmaline's eyes fluttered open. Dull green, distant with pain.

"You… came," she whispered.

"Of course I did," Anya said, her voice breaking. "Always."

Emmaline's hand found hers, weak but certain. "My baby," she rasped, every word a struggle. "The cave."

Anya blinked back tears. "I've got him, Em. I swear—he'll be safe."

"Tell him…" Emmaline coughed, blood speckling her lips. "Tell him I loved him. So much."

Anya gave her hand a gentle squeeze. "He'll know. I promise. He'll know who his mother was."

Emmaline's eyes welled. "You've always been my truest friend. Since the beginning."

Her chest hitched—and then went still.

Anya froze, staring down at her in disbelief. "No… no, no, no. Em?"

She leaned closer, shaking her gently. "Don't you dare do this. Don't leave me."

But Emmaline didn't answer.

Tears spilled freely down Anya's cheeks as she cradled Emmaline's head to her chest. "I'm sorry," she whispered brokenly. "I should've been there. I should've stopped it."

She stayed there for a long moment, letting her grief wash over her. Then, like steel hardening in fire, something shifted.

Anya pressed a kiss to Emmaline's forehead and closed her eyes. "I'll finish what you started," she said quietly. "I'll protect him."

Rising on shaky legs, she gripped Emmaline's rod with white knuckles. Her muscles screamed in protest, but her heart blazed with purpose.

She looked back one final time, her voice a fierce whisper. "He'll live, Em. He'll carry your name—and your strength."

Then she stepped into the night, the flames lighting her path, and the weight of her promise burning just as bright.

PART IV

LORIEN

29

Anya's breath came in ragged gasps as she stumbled through the smoldering ruins, her eyes wide with desperation. Emmaline's final words echoed endlessly in her mind, each anguished syllable driving her forward:

"My baby. The cave."

She pressed a trembling hand to her side, wincing as blistered skin screamed beneath her fingertips. Pain clawed at her consciousness, urging her to collapse, but Anya pushed onward.

"I won't fail you, Em," she whispered, tasting blood and ash. "Not this time."

Memories haunted every step—laughing faces, stolen moments of peace, now reduced to smoke and rubble. Beyond the charred remains of the village, Zol's cavern loomed through the snowstorm, its entrance gaping darkly like a predator's mouth.

Anya crouched low, heart thundering at every rustle and shadow. Miscreants influenced by the darkness could lurk anywhere. Nearing the cavern, a sudden movement caught her eye.

"Focus," she hissed, forcing down panic. "The child is all that matters."

She entered the cavern, instantly frozen by a scent that haunted her darkest nightmares.

"No," she breathed. "It can't be—"

Feathers rustled softly against stone, and the cavern exploded in radiant, sinister light. Lorien stood before her, massive dark wings unfurled, silver eyes glowing like twin moons in a storm. In his arms, he cradled the infant she had come to save.

"Anya," Lorien's voice was velvet over steel—calm, calculating, cold. "Predictable, as always."

Terror rooted her in place, but protective fury surged through her veins. "Give me the child," she demanded, voice trembling despite her determination.

Lorien tilted his head, the movement almost curious. "And why would I? This child is no ordinary soul. I can feel it in his blood—the strength, the lineage. His potential could change the course of fate itself."

Anya's mind flooded with images of her parents' lifeless bodies, her brother's tortured screams—pain Lorien had inflicted without mercy.

"He's just a baby," she snapped. "His mother trusted me. I won't let you take that from her."

Lorien's lips curled faintly, an edge of something resembling... sadness? "She trusted the wrong people."

"You slaughtered my family!" Anya's voice cracked, the memory a fresh wound. "You called it purpose."

"And it was," Lorien said, the hardness returning. "I was trying to prove myself to the gods, Anya. I still am."

A flicker of something else passed through his silver gaze—conflict, perhaps even guilt—but it vanished quickly.

"I made a promise," Anya said, stepping forward. "I'm taking him. You won't stop me."

"You've changed," Lorien said, eyes narrowing. "Not just a scared girl anymore. I respect that."

"And you're still hiding behind power you don't understand."

He stepped closer, voice low. "The gods feared me. Cast me out. Branded me fallen. But I'll prove them wrong. I'll rise again with the gods, not with this darkness that plagues the isle."

Anya blinked, caught off guard. "You're defying the darkness?"

Lorien nodded once. "The darkness believes in order through fear. I believe in legacy. This boy—he could be more than any of us. And maybe... maybe if I help him escape, the gods will see that I am more than what they cast aside. That I still have purpose beyond their judgment. The darkness has decreed the end of humanity—every last human soul purged from this isle." His gaze dropped to the infant. "Yet this little one poses a fascinating problem. Half-human, half-demon—where does he belong in the darkness' perfect world?"

Fear and rage warred within Anya. "It doesn't matter. He deserves a chance."

Lorien's expression hardened. "If I play the darkness's game, I lose what little of myself I have left."

He hesitated, then added quietly, "And because once... you spared me. When you could've struck me down, you didn't."

And that was the worst mistake of her life. Had she let him die then, her family would still be alive. Her coven would still be whole. That single act of mercy had cost her everything.

He handed the child over, slowly. "Take him. Get off the isle. Survive."

Lorien turned his face away. "I'll prove to the gods that I'm not beyond saving. And maybe this time, I can be the one who chooses mercy."

The moment hung heavy between them.

Anya clutched the child tightly, but her eyes burned with rage. "I'll never forgive you," she hissed. "You killed my parents. You claimed my coven. One day, I *will* find a way to end you."

Lorien didn't flinch. His gaze was steady, resigned. "Then let that be your purpose. But go. Now."

Without another word, Anya turned and ran, shadows licking at her heels.

She didn't look back.

Her steps were shaky, breath shallow, but the baby's warmth grounded her. "We'll make it," she murmured. "I promise."

$\mathcal{B}$ehind Anya, fire raged—devouring all that remained. The oppressive heat clawed at her back while acrid smoke stung her eyes, blurring her vision. Tears streamed down her cheeks, mingling with soot and sweat, but she didn't dare slow down. Distant, anguished screams blended with the crackle of flames, a horrific symphony that spurred her onward.

"I won't let you down, Emmaline," she gasped, voice raw. "I swear it."

The baby squirmed and whimpered softly. Anya tightened her hold, forming a protective shield around the precious life entrusted to her.

The forest closed in, ancient trees twisting into monstrous shapes. Gnarled branches reached like claws, trying to trip her. Her muscles screamed in protest, lungs aching with every breath, but she pushed harder. She had to reach the shore—had to find a way off this cursed island.

Memories clawed at her: faces she couldn't save, blood

spilled by her hesitation. But there was no time for guilt. The child's survival was all that mattered now.

Her foot caught a root. She fell. Instinctively, she twisted midair, cradling the baby. Her shoulder hit the ground hard. The baby's piercing cry split the night.

"No, shh," Anya begged, scrambling up. "They'll hear us."

It was too late.

Heavy footsteps thudded behind her. Guttural growls pierced the air. The miscreants had her scent.

Panic surged. She launched forward, adrenaline overriding pain. "I won't let them have you," she whispered fiercely. "I promise."

Emmaline's face swam in her vision—eyes full of love and sorrow. That memory ignited Anya's resolve.

The beasts' snarls drew closer, the air foul with decay and dark magic. Her skin crawled with dread. She'd seen their carnage. She would not become another corpse.

"I won't let them break me," she growled. "I'll fight to my last breath."

The sound of crashing waves spurred her on. The sea—untamed, wild—promised escape.

She burst through the trees. The shoreline stretched ahead, waves roaring. Even as hope flared, dread lingered. The darkness' minions wouldn't stop. Their hunger was endless.

"Hold on," Anya whispered. "We're almost there."

She stumbled onto the sand, legs trembling. Her feet sank, slowing her, but she pressed on. The baby whimpered. Smoke blackened the sky, choking the stars. Her blistered skin throbbed, salt stinging every wound.

She scanned the horizon—nothing. Just endless shore.

Then, it appeared.

A sleek black vessel, forged from dark light, slid through the mist. Its presence was unmistakable—Lorien's magic.

Fear and fury tangled inside her.

The vessel glided to shore as if summoned. Anya hesitated—then climbed aboard, cradling the baby. The boat pulsed beneath her, alive with ancient power.

As it pulled from shore, cutting through black waves, she looked back.

A winged figure hovered above the burning trees, cloaked in smoke and silence.

"You gave us a way out," she whispered bitterly. "But I'll never forgive you."

The baby stirred. Anya looked down at his innocent face and tightened her arms.

The waves rocked the vessel. Sleep came, uneasy and haunted.

In dreams, fire roared. Shadows reached. Whispers hissed lies. Then—light. A golden-haired girl, strange eyes glowing with starlight, stood in shining armor, leading an army. Her voice rang with righteous fury. Emmaline's descendant.

Anya gasped.

The vision wasn't hers alone. The vessel's magic—Lorien's—had shown her. Had he seen the same girl? Had that been why he helped?

She awoke with a start. Dawn painted the sky in soft hues. The sea stretched around them. The child slept, unaware.

Loneliness pressed in. Guilt. Regret. Fear. But the child cooed, anchoring her.

She pressed a kiss to his brow. "We were supposed to leave together, Emmaline. All three of us. But fate had other plans."

Tears brimmed, but she didn't let them fall. The fight wasn't over.

As the boat sailed toward the unknown, Anya steeled herself.
She would protect the child.
She would survive.

31

Anya clutched the baby tightly to her chest, her body trembling from exhaustion as the shadow-forged vessel drifted across the endless sea. Days had passed since she'd fled the cursed isle, and hunger gnawed at her like a ravenous beast. Her lips were cracked, her skin blistered and windburned. Each wave felt like a cruel hand rocking her closer to death.

The baby had stopped crying hours ago, too weak to wail. His tiny body pressed against her—feverish and limp—yet still breathing. She whispered to him constantly, anything to keep his spirit tethered, anything to keep herself from unraveling.

Her gray eyes scanned the endless stretch of water. No land. No food. No hope. If they hadn't been miscreants—unnatural creatures born of shadow and magic—they wouldn't have survived this far. Not the relentless hunger. Not the fire. Not the cursed sea.

Then, as if summoned by desperation itself, a shape emerged through the fog. Large. Silent. Moving.

Anya's heart leapt into her throat. The vessel was massive—

too sleek to be a trader, too clean to be a pirate ship. It glided like a phantom across the sea.

A bell tolled from the ship. Figures appeared on its deck. Ropes were tossed overboard. Voices called out, foreign and sharp, but one word cut through the haze: "Help."

Anya hesitated, her limbs weak and her grip on the child near breaking. She looked down at the baby—barely conscious. If she waited any longer, he wouldn't survive.

With the last shred of strength she possessed, she stood. As her foot left the vessel, its dark frame shimmered, then vanished into mist—gone, as if it had never existed.

Rough hands reached down, firm but not unkind. They hauled her and the baby onto the deck. She collapsed to her knees, the wooden boards solid beneath her for the first time in days.

The baby whimpered, and Anya shielded him instinctively. The sailors gathered, murmuring in confusion.

One stepped forward—a tall man with a weathered face and steady brown eyes.

"You came from the cursed waters," he said, his voice cautious. "No one returns from there."

Anya coughed, her throat raw. She kept her lips tight over her elongated canines. "This child... he's all that's left."

The man knelt beside her. "You're safe now. We're from Eldaraya."

Her brow furrowed. "Eldaraya? I've never heard of it."

That gave the man pause. He glanced back at the others, clearly disturbed. "Never heard of it? Eldaraya is one of the oldest realms in Edros."

She shook her head weakly. "I've never left the place I was raised. Not until now."

"What place?" he asked, frowning. "There's nothing beyond

the cursed waters but myths and storms. No one dares cross them. We thought nothing lived past that veil."

Anya lowered her gaze. She said nothing more. Revealing the existence of the isle was a risk she couldn't take—not when it had been overtaken by horrors most couldn't imagine. If they knew, they might fear her. And if they feared her, they might take the child.

"I don't know who to trust," she whispered.

The man's expression softened. "You don't have to trust us yet. Just let us help you."

She nodded faintly, allowing herself to be guided below deck. The cot was rough, the room dim, but it was shelter. And safety. For the first time in what felt like months, she laid the baby down and knew they would both wake up.

That night, sleep came in fragments, chased by memory and fear. She turned restlessly beneath the thin blanket, haunted not by visions of the future, but by everything she had left behind.

Fire. Screams. Emmaline's bloodied hands. The snarls of the miscreants in the dark.

Anya jolted awake, her skin slick with sweat. Her heart thundered. But there were no dreams this time, no messages carried on shadowed magic. Just silence—and the crushing weight of survival.

She wiped her mouth, felt the familiar edge of her fangs against her wrist. She would need to be careful now—keep them hidden, say little, avoid suspicion.

A knock came at her door.

The captain stepped in, eyes cautious. "You need to come topside," he said. "We're approaching the shores of Eldaraya. The king will want to see you himself."

She gathered the baby, heart pounding. "Why?"

"Because you crossed the cursed waters and lived. Because

you carry something—someone—the king must know about. There's already talk among the crew. Whispers."

Anya said nothing. She followed him up, the baby swaddled in her arms, her lips carefully pressed together.

As the ship cut through the final stretch of sea, Eldaraya rose into view—white cliffs, towering spires, sunlight gleaming off golden banners. It was beautiful. Peaceful. And for the first time in what felt like forever, it looked like a place untouched by shadow.

Hope stirred in her chest, fragile but undeniable.

She glanced down at the baby, brushing a soot-smudged finger across his cheek. He stirred slightly, letting out a small, contented sigh. Maybe this could be a beginning—not just an escape.

Still, doubt whispered at the edges of her mind. If the king discovered the truth of what she was... of what followed her through the veil of cursed waters... he might not offer refuge.

He might see her as a threat.

And if he chose to send her back?

Anya held the baby closer, her fangs aching behind closed lips. No. She wouldn't let that happen.

But for now, she let herself believe. Just for a moment. That maybe, just maybe, they had a future here.

She looked toward the golden shore and whispered, "Let this be enough."

The sky above the isle was a canvas of stormclouds, streaked with veins of lightning that never quite touched the ground. Lorien stood at the edge of the obsidian cliff, his ash gray wings outstretched, catching the wind that howled from the sea. The destruction behind him was old now, buried beneath vines and silence, but the land still remembered. So did he.

He had watched Anya escape. Had felt the moment the child crossed the veil into safety, wrapped in magic of his making. He had seen the future shimmer behind his closed eyes—a girl clad in light and ice, leading a battle not yet born.

But that vision had faded. And now, all that remained was the wait.

Lorien clenched his fists, the divine magic in his blood pulsing like a second heartbeat. He had refused the darkness. He had not knelt to it, nor bowed to the ruin the miscreants brought. The gods thought casting him down would break him.

Instead, it had forged him.

He looked to the heavens, to the place that had once been his home. The stars offered no answers. They never did. But one day, they would see him again—not as a fallen, not as a weapon—but as a force reborn.

A voice, low and gravelled, curled around him from the shadows. "Still waiting for redemption?"

Lorien didn't turn. "Redemption was never the goal. Understanding is."

The shadow laughed—a sound like metal scraping stone. "You think helping the girl makes you worthy? That child was marked for death. By Conivx's will, he was never meant to leave the isle."

"And yet," Lorien replied coolly, "he did."

The shadow surged closer, its form filled with menace. "You disobeyed her. Do you truly think she will spare you?"

"I don't serve her. I never have." Lorien's wings flared, catching the light of the distant moon. "I serve purpose. And that child—his bloodline—serves a greater one than any of you understand."

"You've made an enemy of us all."

Lorien finally turned, silver eyes glowing with divine defiance. "Good. Let them come. I have no fear of shadows. I've lived among them too long to be swallowed now."

The shadow recoiled slightly, its edges flickering like dying flame.

"I won't kneel to your chaos," Lorien said. "I will rise. And when the gods see what I've built, they will regret casting me down."

He stepped from the cliff, wings catching the wind, rising higher until the isle was no more than a scar on the horizon.

He flew not to conquer, but to prepare.

Because when the girl came—the descendant born of ice and fate—she would need more than power.

She would need him.

And this time, he would not fail.

Let the gods watch. Let them judge.

He would write the next chapter himself.

Dive into the tale of Airella—a fierce warrior burdened by prophecy, hunted by monsters, and drawn to a man with secrets in his blood. As darkness rises and the forgotten past claws its way into the light, destiny and desire will collide.

Keep reading for a preview of
ISLE OF BEASTS AND SHADOWS

256 YEARS LATER

ISLE OF BEASTS AND SHADOWS

Airella's world shattered when the plague took her father, leaving her to navigate life at just seven years old. With her mother battling a chronic illness, she became their anchor, shouldering the weight of survival. By eighteen, the burden of providing for her small family—her ailing mother and her spirited younger brother, Arii—had only grown heavier.

Arii dashed down the narrow hallway of their cottage, his untamed blond hair bouncing with each step. Airella watched him with a mix of exasperation and fondness.

"Arii, it's too early, and you stink." She wrinkled her nose. "When was your last bath? What trouble have you gotten into this time?"

"I was practicing my sword skills," he declared proudly. "I'm going to be the best swordsman in all of Edros."

"Arii," Airella's voice softened, though her words were firm. "We've talked about this."

"I know, I know. But how else will I protect you and Mama

from the villains?" he asked with the unwavering determination of an eleven-year-old.

"That's my job," she reminded him, ruffling his hair. "Papa's weapons stay locked away. Lay a hand on them again, and you'll be eating pig slop for dinner."

"No, please don't!" Arii whined, dashing off. Airella chuckled, shaking her head. He had once dared to taste pig slop out of curiosity—it had not ended well.

Stepping into her room, Airella caught her reflection in the small, cracked mirror. Her mismatched eyes—one icy blue, the other a vivid emerald green—stared back at her, a stark reminder of the father she missed dearly. His teachings, his wisdom, his unwavering love—gone. But she still had Arii. She still had her mother. And she would protect them at any cost.

The floorboards creaked under her weight as she moved toward her nightstand. The cottage was crumbling around them, a victim of time and poverty. A rusty tin can in the center of the room collected water from a leaking ceiling, a reminder of the storm that had battered their home the night before. No matter how hard she worked, there was never enough money for repairs.

Winter had made everything worse. The animals had gone into hibernation, making hunting nearly impossible. With fewer hides to sell at the market, their already meager funds were dwindling. The thought of turning to desperate means lingered in the back of her mind, but she quickly shoved it away. There had to be another way.

A sudden knock at the door made her jump.

"Yes?" she called, her pulse quickening.

The bedroom door creaked open, revealing her mother's frail figure. Elizabeth's once-bright eyes were clouded with exhaustion, her illness weighing heavily on her.

"Airella," her mother's voice was barely above a whisper, "they're outside… They're coming."

Dread settled in Airella's stomach like a stone.

"Who?" she asked, stepping closer.

Elizabeth's eyes filled with urgency. "Listen to me, child. There are things you do not yet understand. Take your father's axe. It will protect you."

Airella's breath caught in her throat.

Before she could question her mother further, the sharp command of men's voices cut through the air, followed by the crash of their front door being forced open.

Panic surged through her as Elizabeth shoved a golden, dual-bladed battle axe into her trembling hands.

"There is no time," her mother said, voice shaking. "Hide! I'll find Arii."

Airella barely had time to react before Elizabeth pushed her away, locking the door behind her. Footsteps pounded against the wooden floor, accompanied by harsh orders barked by men who had no right to be there.

Clutching the axe, Airella crouched behind her bed, heart hammering. The weapon was heavy, its jeweled handle glinting even in the dim light. She had never wielded Dawnbreaker before. Her father's most prized possession. A weapon of legend. Now, it was all she had.

"No, don't hurt him!" her mother's voice rang out, raw with desperation.

Airella's blood ran cold at the response.

"Then tell us where the girl is. If we don't find her, the boy will suffice."

"No," another voice interjected, sharper, crueler. "We need the one who takes after their father."

Airella's hands clenched around the axe handle. They knew. They knew about her.

"Search the house," the leader commanded. "Burn it down if you have to."

Airella barely had time to steel herself before the door to her room burst open. Boots stomped inside. She held her breath as shadows passed over the floorboards.

Just when she thought they might leave, a hand clamped around her ankle and yanked her out from under the bed.

"Let go of me!" she snarled, kicking and thrashing. With reckless strength, she swung Dawnbreaker, narrowly missing her captor's head. The blade lodged deep into the wooden floorboards instead.

The soldier staggered but didn't let go. More hands grabbed her, pinning her arms and forcing her onto her feet.

Bursting into the main room, her heart twisted at the sight before her—Arii in a soldier's grasp, struggling, and her mother kneeling before their intruders, her face a mask of fear and defiance.

"Wait! Don't hurt them!" Airella cried. "What is the meaning of this?"

Another soldier stepped forward, unfurling an aged parchment. His uniform bore the crest of Eldaraya. His voice rang with unshakable authority as he read:

"Airella Devereaux. By decree of the King of Eldaraya, you are to be promptly escorted to the palace. Any resistance will be met with force."

Airella struggled harder, her fury blinding. "You can't just take me!"

The soldiers paid her no mind. One hoisted her over his shoulder as if she weighed nothing. She screamed and kicked, but their grip was ironclad.

Outside, villagers peered from their homes, watching in stunned silence as she was dragged away. The relentless downpour mixed with her tears, her golden locks heavy with rain.

Her mother's voice cut through the storm. "Hold on to it, Airella!"

Airella turned her head just in time to see a soldier carrying Dawnbreaker away. Her heart clenched. She wasn't just losing her freedom—she was losing everything.

Lightning split the sky, thunder roaring in her ears as she was forced into a waiting carriage. The door slammed shut, sealing her fate.

And as the wheels began to roll, she realized—there was no one left to protect her family now.

ACKNOWLEDGMENTS

To write a book is to journey through shadows and light—and this one, *Isle of Lies and Legends*, was born in the darkest corners of heartbreak, ambition, and legacy.

First and foremost, thank you to my readers. Whether you've followed this saga from *Isle of Beasts and Shadows* or this is your first time setting foot on the Forgotten Isle, your love for these broken characters and twisted tales means more to me than I can ever say. You make this world breathe.

To my family—thank you for always believing in me, even when I doubted myself. Your support has been my constant light.

To Cristian, my love and anchor: thank you for your patience during the late nights, emotional rewrites, and chaotic ideas I had to talk out loud at random hours. You've seen every side of this story and still encourage me to chase the next one.

To my best friends (you know who you are), thank you for cheering me on, reading early drafts, and reminding me why I started writing in the first place. Your honesty, hype, and sometimes brutal feedback shaped this book into something far better than it began.

To Haley, my podcast partner-in-crime and fellow bookish baddie—thank you for inspiring me with your passion, your humor, and your unwavering encouragement. Thank you for being the very first to dive into this book. Your feedback gave it shape. Your notes made it stronger. This journey has been all the more magical with you in it.

To the incredible indie author and book community—thank you for showing up, supporting one another, and proving that there is power in storytelling and strength in solidarity. This industry can be brutal, but together, we rise.

And finally, to the girls like Conivx—the ones who've been overlooked, underestimated, or cast aside: your story matters, even when it's messy. Especially when it's messy.

This is for the liars, the legends, and the ones who were never meant to survive.

With love and shadows,

McCayleigh Daniels

ABOUT THE AUTHOR

McCayleigh is a Texas-based author, voice actor, and lover of all things fantasy. As a proud Texas A&M University former student, she's all about that Aggie spirit. Gig 'em!

When she's not writing epic tales of romance and adventure, she lends her voice to characters in audiobooks, bringing stories to life with her rich, captivating narration.

She enjoys spending time with her husband Cristian and their two beloved Shih Tzus, Chewy and Leia. She also shares her home with a sulcata tortoise who keeps life grounded amid her creative flights of fancy.

McCayleigh is dedicated to telling empowering, female-led stories within the realms of fantasy and romance. She hopes her work inspires readers to embrace their inner strength, fight for what they believe in, and never stop believing in magic.

FOLLOW THE AUTHOR

To stay up to date on future books, announcements, and exclusive content, visit www.mccayleighdaniels.com.

Don't forget to follow McCayleigh on social media for the latest news, giveaways, sneak peeks, and behind-the-scenes updates.

Instagram, Threads, & TikTok: @mccayleighdaniels

PLEASE LEAVE A REVIEW

Thank you so much for joining me on this adventure through Isle of Lies and Legends. If you enjoyed this story, I would greatly appreciate it if you could take a moment to leave a review. Your feedback not only helps me grow as an author but also helps other readers discover the book. Reviews are incredibly important in spreading the word, and your support means the world to me.

Where you can review:
 Goodreads
 Amazon
 Barnes & Noble
 Books-A-Million
 Storygraph
 and more!

Don't forget to share your review on social media using the hashtag #IsleOfLiesAndLegends.

Thank you for being part of this journey!

TRIGGER WARNINGS

- **Death and Murder** (including family members and children)
- **Abuse and Manipulation** (psychological and magical)
- **Toxic/Controlling Relationships**
- **Gaslighting**
- **Betrayal by Loved Ones**
- **Sexual Content** (emotionally intense; not graphic)
- **Violence and Bloodshed** (battle scenes, attacks, magical combat)
- **Dark Magic and Occult Themes**
- **Parental Abandonment / Complicated Family Dynamics**
- **Destruction of Homes/Villages**
- **Mental Instability / Emotional Turmoil**
- **Mentions of Pregnancy and Loss**

Please be mindful of these elements before continuing, and take care while reading.